KU-152-630

The Shootout at Dogleg Crossing

Journalist Peter Lomass is enjoying a break from work, travelling and revisiting old haunts, when he discovers a poem entitled 'The Shootout at Dogleg Crossing' on a newspaper clipping from twenty years earlier, pinned up in a hotel reception area. He decides to trace the origins of the poem and his quest takes him deep into Mexico, where Pete finds himself mixed up in all sorts of skulduggery and danger.

By the same author

The Pinfire Lady
The Pinfire Lady Strikes Back

The Shootout at Dogleg Crossing

P.J. Gallagher

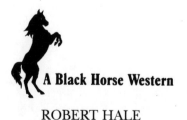

A Black Horse Western

ROBERT HALE

© P.J. Gallagher 2019
First published in Great Britain 2019

ISBN 978-0-7198-3039-6

The Crowood Press
The Stable Block
Crowood Lane
Ramsbury
Marlborough
Wiltshire SN8 2HR

www.bhwesterns.com

Robert Hale is an imprint
of The Crowood Press

The right of P.J. Gallagher to be identified as
author of this work has been asserted by him
in accordance with the Copyright, Designs and
Patents Act 1988

All rights reserved. No part of this publication may be
reproduced or transmitted in any form or by any means,
electronic or mechanical, including photocopying, recording,
or any information storage and retrieval system, without
permission in writing from the publishers.

DUNDEE CITY
COUNCIL

LOCATION
ARTHURSTONE

ACCESSION NUMBER
CO10028 4247

SUPPLIER | PRICE
ASK | £14.50

CLASS No. | DATE
82391 | 27/2/20

Typeset by
Derek Doyle & Associates, Shaw Heath
Printed and bound in Great Britain by
4Bind Ltd, Stevenage, SG1 2XT

Dedicated to my Alabama friends
Jim and Caroline Mitchell

CHAPTER ONE

The Shootout at Dogleg Crossing

Now Red's Saloon was full of noise, the crowd was
   going wild,
As Jenny Ling stood up to sing – she was a winsome
   child.
With a voice so clear, it brought a tear to miners and
   cowhands alike,
But one face just wore a sneer – 'twas the gambler
   'Dapper Mike'.
'Yu fools!' he cried, as he flipped a card, 'Yu'd think
   she's from heaven above.
When all's said an' done, when the singing is sung,
She's naught but a common soiled dove!'

The boys of the Bar 6 were there that night – just paid
   and loaded for bear,
An' at Dapper Mike's cry, they turned as one, with
   looks as would whiten your hair.
'Take back them words 'bout this maiden fair, or as
   sure as we're a tootin'

We'll give you thirty seconds to make amends, an' then
     we're startin' shootin'!'
Mike sprang to his feet, hand on his gun, 'Take back
     my words. I'll never!
A fight? Yu'll find I'm not alone!' That wily Mike was
     clever,
By bribes and drinks he'd bought a gang. That's how
     the work was done,
An' the Bar 6 boys stared around the room, outnumbered
     five to one.

There was a frozen moment of time that night. An'
     then a pistol roared,
Nobody knew who fired the shot, that slammed into a
     board.
But the shootin' kinda became general then, all kinds
     of firearms spoke,
Pistols, rifles, shotgun, all added noise an' lots of
     smoke,
Bar lights were smashed, a chandelier crashed, in the
     midst of that hellish room,
While the weaponry cracked, an' the muzzle blasts
     flashed, all thru' the gathering gloom.

The shootin' spread to the street outside, midst the
     horses at the rail,
An' the broncos reared and neighed in fright, along
     with a woman's wail.
Red's Saloon was now on fire, but the shootin' did not
     cease,
Both sides had a mind to win, an' nobody cried for peace.

A group made a stand at the Mercantile. Were they
    cowboys four?
A kerosene lamp set the store on fire, as they left
    through the rear door.

The fires spread from side to side – the Bon Ton Café
    and the bank,
By dawn every building was ablaze, an' the air was
    chokin' an' stank.
The shootin' had dwindled as hours passed, to a
    number of solitary duels,
The last took place on the edge of town, in a corral
    housing Ezra's mules.
The only one left of the Bar 6 boys was the foreman
    named Bill Syke,
While facin' him across the yard was the man known
    as Dapper Mike.

They drew as one, their pistols roared – then again,
    an' yet another round,
Mike bit the dust with mortal wounds, his life blood
    spread on the ground.
Bill sank to his knees, his wounds were grave, he
    thought his time was nigh.
When thru' the smoke came a figure trim. 'Twas Jenny
    Ling passing by,
'Oh Bill! So ill! I do declare! Of that crowd – you were
    the most nice,
When you are well an' feelin' swell, see me – I'll just
    charge you half price!'

The work was unsigned, not even by that international scribbler Anonymous or his colleague A.N. Other.

Perhaps I should introduce myself. Lomass is the name, Pete Lomass. By profession I'm an international correspondent or if you like, a roving reporter. In my early working days I was a travelling salesman with a varied line of products that helped me make my way through college. My first job as a reporter was with *The Rocky Mountain News* in Denver. I stayed with them for a couple of years and then worked for the *Atlanta Gazette*, gradually becoming known for my reporting of hot spots all over the globe.

Over the years I reported on wars in South Africa and Europe; was with Kitchener's lot when they went up the Nile; was with Teddy Roosevelt at San Juan Hill and in China during the Boxer affair.

Now, my paper had given me a six-month furlough – with pay – and I was just enjoying travelling through areas I had visited twenty years earlier.

A sudden typical southern downpour had driven me into a rather run-down building, which described itself a trifle grandiloquently as The Grand Hotel.

The musty reception area was deserted apart from the long-lingering odour of tobacco and sour alcohol. I rang the bell and awaiting a response, wandered around the room glancing at the notices of bygone cattle sales and social events. My attention had been drawn to a piece of newsprint held by two thumbtacks. It was the poem 'The Shootout at Dogleg Crossing'. Taking out my reporter's note pad, I had rapidly jotted the words down.

My musing on the origin of the poem was abruptly interrupted. 'Hey mister, you looking for a drink or a bed or something?'

I turned to behold a male figure of indeterminate age surveying me from behind the desk counter. He apologized for not answering the bell sooner but explained that he'd been cleaning out the hen-house, a fact made obvious by the wisps of straw in his hair. The storm had passed on but, since it was late afternoon and still raining, I decided to rent a room for the night.

I signed the register as 'Peter Lomass, Tourist', which raised an eyebrow from the desk clerk and he told me that as the only guest I could have any room in the house. Supper was to be served at six o'clock, with coffee available in the morning. The bar meanwhile was open now if I wished to irrigate, said he hopefully.

I answered in the affirmative, asking for a shot of rye and inviting him to have one with me. He complied willingly and we spoke together for a while regarding the usual generalities, the weather, business, the economy and life in general. Then, pointing to the newspaper poem pinned to the wall, I enquired as to the author and from whence did it come.

11

'Well, sir, I don't rightly know. It was up there when I bought the old hotel so I just left it up there with the other stuff. As to who wrote it, your guess is as good as mine. I'm sorry. I just don't know.'

I stayed one night. The room was clean, the bed likewise although the mattress was lumpy. The evening meal was plain, but surprisingly appetizing, and the company, the hotelier and his wife and two ranchers, was affable.

I suspect that I must have been considered unsociable, as I was a trifle short in my answers, and contributed little to the general conversation. The problem was that I was seized by an overpowering desire to find out more about the author of the doggerel on the wall, and indeed about the incidents depicted.

Casting my mind back to the time when I had been a salesman, I thought hard, and realized that it must now be nigh on twenty-two years since I had actually been in Dogleg. I recalled a saloon owned by a cheery Irishman, who looked askance at the skinny kid who came in boldly and asked for a beer. But he never asked how old I was and drew a foaming mug full of brew as I placed my nickel on the scarred counter.

The fringe of gingery red hair still clinging to his near-bald pate indicated the origin of his nickname, Red Michael Corcoran, otherwise known as Red. Adjacent to the saloon there was a small café, the name escapes me but I recall that it was run by two of the nicest, prettiest girls in Texas, who made each customer feel he was something special. To sit at one of those little round tables, covered by a blue and white check table cloth, and be served by one of those gorgeous girls was one of the high points of my salesman's career.

There was a small bank with a single teller who reluctantly changed a twenty-dollar bill for a young stranger, but only after handing said bill to the head teller, accountant, manager, bank president, or whatever title was used by the other person present. Facing the bank was a large general store, The Mercantile, whose owner adamantly had informed me that no, he most certainly did not want a beautifully bound edition of *Our Family Physician,* not even for resale. On the other hand, the elderly gent at the livery stable was interested in, and had bought, *The Complete Book of the Horse.* He confessed to me that he couldn't read, but liked looking at books with pictures.

All in all, Dogleg was a nice quiet little town; so quiet in fact that they didn't even have a sheriff. One of the locals confided in me as to how the town got its name.

'Well, it was right alongside the Mojave River and there was a ford there. But you daresn't make a bee line for the other bank when crossing because of quicksands. The traveller had to make a turn in midstream, a dogleg to arrive safely on the other side.'

Thus I pondered as I wished the rest of the table folk good night and prepared for bed. I started thinking. *You know, I've got time. I don't have anyone waiting for me. Why don't I just mosey on westward and do a bit of searching around the Dogleg area and try to get the true story and also the author of the poem? What do I need? Well, some basic provisions in case I am living rough. A pot for coffee and a skillet. Tin plate and mug and knife, fork and spoon. A poncho and blanket if sleeping under the stars.* I fell asleep still planning my expedition.

The following morning I obtained the supplies and gear that I needed for my trek. Noticing a series of leather holsters hanging on the wall prompted a new line of thought. In my grip was an 1878 model, double action Frontier Colt of 45 calibre with the barrel cut back to six inches. I decided to purchase an open holster and fifty more cartridges. I did not think it would be out of place since, in Texas, many men still openly carried handguns. Piling all my purchases in the flivver, I proceeded westward.

Two days and three tyre punctures later I was in Langtry where, until a couple of years ago, Judge Roy Bean had held court. Langtry was where it was said 'there was no law west of the Pecos'. When I travelled through, the town had a population of less than a hundred and consisted of two saloons, a Railroad Depot, and a general store. In the latter establishment I made a lucky find. Somehow, the store had, by mistake probably, received a consignment of heavy truck tyres which would fit the rims of my car, especially if we removed the mud guards. A local mechanic got to work and when I left town I had the satisfaction that, hopefully, there would be no punctures. Two hundred miles to go!

Before I had reached Langtry I had filled the loops of my cartridge belt and taken to wearing my holstered revolver. Initially, I felt self-conscious and was sure folks were looking at me, but nobody seemed to care and soon it became part of my dress routine. Now, as I travelled even further west into sparsely inhabited territory, there was comfort in having the means to defend myself and also in knowing that to a certain extent, I had the skills to do so.

The highway had long since degenerated into a potholed, rut-filled track as I drove carefully on, gripping the steering wheel, while the car bucked and twisted beneath me. The countryside was a kind of semi-desert with the odd Joshua tree, yucca plants, and other assorted cacti decorating the wilderness. The occasional dwelling I observed was, invariably, a single storied adobe building, around which in some cases an optimistic owner had attempted to scratch out a vegetable garden.

Finally, a track leading off to the right and a sign hand-painted on a warped piece of board nailed to a post, leaning drunkenly in the right direction, announced that Dogleg was three miles ahead. Sure enough as my faithful Ford rose above the next incline, I could see ahead in the far distance the shape of buildings. So Dogleg, like the phoenix, had apparently risen from the ashes.

CHAPTER TWO

We drew nearer and the buildings began to take on definite individual shapes. They were all single storey and mostly seemed to be made with an adobe finish. That in itself was different from the former town. At that time, the town, like most in the old West, had wooden-frame buildings, with at least two rising to a second floor.

The present town was much smaller, consisting of no more than thirty or forty adobes, scattered seemingly in a haphazard fashion on either side of the track that constituted Main Street. Noticing that one building had the word 'Cantina' emblazoned across the front I halted and, happy to stretch my legs, got down and entered the cool, darkened interior of the cantina – a sharp contrast to the glare of the noonday sun.

As my eyes grew accustomed to the lighting I noticed that, apart from the patron behind the bar and two Mexicans engaged in a quiet game of chess, the cantina was empty. I approached the bar and the patron greeted me with a raised bottle and a query, 'Tequila, Señor?'

I shook my head regretfully. 'No thank you, Señor. I am much too thirsty. Do you have any beer? American beer?'

He replied '*Sí* Señor,' and diving under the counter, produced a bottle of Coors dripping wet from the water in which it had been cooling. He produced a moderately clean glass and decanted the golden liquid, gently yet with a nice head of foaming bubbles. Apologetically, he said, 'That will be fifty cents, Señor. I'm sorry it is so expensive but it is difficult to get it here.'

I gladly put two quarters on the counter and then, feeling generous, added yet another as I took a long swallow of the welcome brew. It slid down my throat beautifully and I had just raised my glass for yet another swig when there was an interruption.

A large figure darkened the entrance. Seconds later, a man in range gear was standing at the bar saying, 'Gimme a bottle of beer, Pablo. My throat is so dry it's touching my backbone!'

Pablo spread his hands apologetically, 'I am sorry Señor Rossiter. I have no more American beer. This gentleman,' indicating me, 'bought the last bottle!'

I attempted to placate the newcomer. 'Look, I've only had two drinks out of this bottle. If you like we can share the remainder.'

He glanced at the bottle and then, ignored me, choosing instead to bellow at poor Pablo, screaming that *his beer* had been sold to some goddamn stranger. He put his hand on the gun at his hip and I suddenly decided that this had gone far enough. I drew my Colt and levelled it at Rossiter.

'Just keep your hands away from your gun, mister! Now place them flat on the bar!'

He did as ordered, although I could tell that he was inwardly seething.

'Now let's just settle down and not let this go any further. I offered to share my bottle with you and so far you have not given me the courtesy of a reply. We'll leave that for a moment. Did you have your name on that bottle? If so I'd pay you for it. If not you have no right to demand that this man has to reserve certain brands just for your pleasure. What do you say? Shall we forget the whole affair and shake hands like gentlemen?' and I transferred my pistol to my left hand and stuck out the right paw, offering it in friendship.

His negative response was not quite what I had expected. He literally curled his upper lip in disdain and, with a muttered 'Bah!' he brushed my hand aside and stalked out of the cantina.

Pablo exhaled his breath just like a collapsing balloon. 'Thank you, Señor. I am very much afraid that Jeem Rossiter he is like the volcano. She explode suddenly, and nobody knows what will happen next.'

Then he made a startling statement, 'I do not think that I want that Rossiter for my son-in-law, but. . .' he paused, 'my Juanita she insists they are in love. What can a father do?'

I commiserated with him on the trials of fatherhood and took my leave, having first obtained

19

directions to the town's Boot Hill, which was about a quarter of a mile away to the northeast. Pablo himself knew very little of the earlier history of the town, having only been in the area a little over five years.

I drove out to the cemetery as directed and strolled around. Like all such places, it was a sad, desolate location in which to have one's final rest. Few of the graves had either a stone or iron monument. Most had merely a sagging cross or an upright slab of wood inscribed with the usual details. Name, date of birth, date of death, and frequently a biblical verse or comment, 'Gone but not forgotten' being the most frequent.

Wandering around I finally found a name that I recognized; 'Michael (Red) Corcoran, Born Co. Mayo, Ireland 1840, Died 1887. R.I.P.' So it looked as though Red Corcoran must have died during or shortly after the shootout which destroyed the town.

When driving through Dogleg I had noticed a large sign 'EATS' over the doorway of one building and, feeling the need for a meal cooked by someone other than myself, I drove down from Boot Hill and parking my flivver, entered the Eatery.

Finding a free table, I sat down and awaited service. The place appeared to be quite busy since it was early evening, and was doing a good trade with individuals and couples occupying most of the tables.

Eventually, a buxom middle-aged lady approached my table and greeted me with a smile saying, 'Howdy stranger! What'll it be?' as she placed a soiled menu in front of me. Glancing quickly over the bill of fare I ordered fried chicken with mashed 'taters and vegetables (in season), hot biscuits and coffee.

With a cry of 'Comin' right up!' she whisked away the menu card and moments later reappeared with a large mug of steaming hot coffee. 'Your dinner will be up directly. Just holler if you need more coffee.' And off she went again.

I thanked her as she retreated and cautiously sipped at the coffee. Something was bothering me and I couldn't put my finger on it. That lady? Did I feel that I knew her? Could it possibly be one of the girls who had captivated me on my last visit to Dogleg? Twenty odd years had passed. She would have filled out but was still not unsightly. As far as I could guess she was about the same height. Brown hair with a trace of grey? Well, that was true of both of us!

My reverie was interrupted by the lady in person, bearing a tray on which was the meal that I had ordered. 'There you are, stranger! Get that inside you and you won't need anything more until breakfast.'

I thanked her and then as she turned away said, 'Excuse me, ma'am! Have we met before?'

She turned back with a puzzled look on her face and I continued hurriedly, 'I'm not trying to be forward, but I'm just wondering if we ever met in the long distant past. Did you work at the Bon Ton Café before the fire?' She gasped and then silently nodded her head. 'I was right! You served me, a skinny young lad, and I never forgot you!'

I took a chance. 'Would it be OK for me to interview you about that episode? I'm doing a story about the Dogleg fire and I need to speak to folks who were there at the time.'

She shook her head, 'Not now, I'm far too busy. We're open until nine o'clock and then I need about a half hour to clean up. I'll meet you out front at nine-thirty and we'll find somewhere to talk.'

I spent the rest of the day fixing up accommodation for myself in the closest thing in town to a hotel, a bar that had two or three rooms in the rear of the building available to rent, and a shed where I housed my machine. Then, after killing some time nursing a couple of drinks at the bar, I strolled the length of the boardwalk and back, killing time until nine-thirty.

CHAPTER THREE

I was curious as to the outcome of the meeting we had arranged. Meeting a totally strange woman in a strange town, late at night, for most men would be for only one purpose, which would also frequently be the intention of the female part of the equation, whereas my purpose was merely to further my quest for information.

Nine-thirty came and went. Nobody appeared. I figured she had thought better of my request when the door to the café opened and she slipped out, locking the door behind her.

'Sorry I'm late. There was a lot of cleaning up to do today.' She paused, obviously thinking for a moment. 'Would you mind coming along to my place?' She chuckled quietly. 'I assure you. Your reputation will remain quite intact! It's just that it is difficult to find a place where we won't be interrupted.'

I murmured my agreement and she took my offered arm as we walked away from the main street to a little cottage lit up purely by the light of a full moon. Once inside, she lit an oil lamp and turning up the wick, revealed a comfortably appointed living room with a small kitchen in an alcove and, through an archway, what appeared to be a bedroom.

'Take a seat, Mr Lomass! I'll be with you in a minute!' she said as she vanished into the bedroom, drawing a curtain across the opening behind her. I heard the rustle of feminine clothing as she was obviously changing from her work attire. Not, I hoped, into the clichéd 'something more comfortable'.

Now how did she know my name I pondered, and what else did she know?

She reappeared wearing a loose floral dress and smiled down at me with her right hand extended.

'First, introductions. My name is Jane Bronson. I'm thirty-eight years old and I am the sole owner of the Eatery, where you had dinner. There was no magic involved in finding out who you are. I just sent someone along to the bar where you had rented a room and he returned with the information. As to your occupation, over the years I have read many of your articles and, quite frankly, I've enjoyed most of your stuff. Now, what is a famous reporter doing in an out-of-the-way place such as Dogleg?'

I produced my handwritten copy of 'The Shootout at Dogleg Crossing' and passed it to Jane. 'Are you familiar with this? If so, is it an accurate description of events and who wrote it?'

She took my notebook and read the indicated page carefully. And I could not help noticing that, as

24

she did so, her hands were shaking. A natural tired reflex, or was it bringing to mind things past and best forgotten?

At length, Jane lowered the book and sighed deeply, and I noticed tears glistening in the corners of her eyes. She noticed my concern and turned away for a moment before saying, 'I'm all right, Mr Lomass. Yes! Allowing for poetic licence, I would say that the majority of the poem is correct, although there are important things omitted. Perhaps we could start by me telling you of events as I remember that night.'

She settled down in the other armchair and closed her eyes. 'You will recall that Dogleg was a busy berg at that time. Far more active than today. Cattle prices were sky high, and the ranchers were making lots of money and hiring more hands. There was talk of a rail link eastward to Langtry and that created a business boom. To add to the prosperity, silver had been discovered in the hills to the west and, therefore, we had an influx of miners in town.

'My sister Beth and I had pooled our capital, such as it was, and opened our little eatery, The Bon Ton Café, and we were doing a good, steady business with all manner of folks. Well, as the poem states, it was payday, not only for many of the cowboys but also for a number of miners, and in those days the town was wide open.

'From the café, as we cleaned up after a busy day, we could hear the whooping and yelling coming from Red's saloon. The noise would rise to a crescendo as each new performer took his or her place on the rickety stage at the end of the barroom, and then drop to almost nothing as the singing or act commenced.

'In the case of the Ling girl, of course not being there, I just don't know exactly what happened. All of a sudden shots rang out and then more shots, obviously from different weapons, since the sounds were different. There were yells and screams and, from the side windows of the café which faced the saloon, we saw a spreading red glow which got ever larger.

'The saloon crowd stampeded trying to escape the flames and poured out into Main Street, still discharging their guns, either at the sky in drunken jollity, or taking advantage of the mayhem to shoot at people for past, real or imagined grievances. You have no idea Mr Lomass! It was absolutely awful!

'We were lying on the floor. Bullets had already smashed two of our windows when Beth stood up. I'm not sure what she intended to do and will never know. At that moment our front door opened and a figure stood there. Beth recognized the man and called a greeting, as she did so he opened fire, the bullets knocking my sister back so she fell over me. He left and dear Beth died in my arms. I dragged her body out of the rear door of the café as the front of the building went up in flames, and we lay there while the town burned.

'Yes, Mr Lomass! I remember that night very well. It is burned indelibly into my very being and, someday, that man who shot my sister, even though it

26

may have been in a drunken frenzy, will pay the price for his evil act!'

She fell silent and we both sat there while she remained with her head bowed, sobbing quietly over her sister murdered so many years ago. At length, feeling uncomfortable at the way the interview had proceeded and realizing that, indirectly, I was more than a little responsible for recreating the sadness Jane was experiencing, I rose to take my leave.

'Don't go, Mr Lomass! I'll be all right in a moment. I thought that I'd shed all my tears over the shooting of Beth long ago. I was wrong, but I'm over it now.'

I smiled at her and suggested that as I had been addressing her as Jane rather than as Miss Bronson, since I had observed that she did not wear a wedding ring, perhaps she would call me Peter, or better still Pete, as that had been my handle for years.

I looked at my watch and noticing that it was close to midnight, indicated that it was time that I left and proposed that, if it was not too painful perhaps we could have another discussion. Jane agreed and we formally shook hands as I opened the door to leave.

As I did so, there was a sudden flame out in the darkness and a bullet buried itself in the door post, followed by the heavy report of a pistol shot. I reacted instinctively, drawing my Colt as I dropped to the floor, simultaneously telling Jane to put out the light. A second shot entered the adobe wall to my right and I triggered two shots in the direction of the muzzle flame of the would-be assassin's gun. Then there was silence. After whispering to Jane not to put the lamp on yet, I ran crouching and zigzagging to the location from whence the shots had come.

The shots had awakened the neighbourhood and several people, among whom was the town marshal, came to find out who was causing the disturbance. Asking the latter to remain, I fended off the other people by intimating that I thought that some characters were merely celebrating July 4th a couple of weeks too early.

Mollified, they left and I introduced myself to Al Watson, the marshal, and together we examined the door post and the wall in which the shots were embedded. Jane joined us and very tactfully explained the reason for me being at her cottage so late at night.

Al was a relative newcomer to Dogleg, having been appointed by the town council four years ago. He of course knew of the fire, but only in a general sort of way, and intimated that the shooting that night was hardly to be connected with an event that had happened more than twenty years ago.

He left and, after exacting a promise from Jane that she would keep her door locked and also that we would meet again the following evening, I bade her goodnight and walked home in a pensive yet alert manner.

Reaching the saloon I went through to my room, got ready for bed, and sat down for a last cigarette as I pondered a while over the events of the last few hours. Who would have wanted to shoot me? I was damned sure that those two shots were no accident, despite what I had told the curious enquirers. The only person who had exhibited any animosity was that fella Jim Rossiter in the cantina and I couldn't see a single bottle of beer being the cause of mayhem.

I was also curious about my own reaction. It was not the first time that I had been under fire. After all, when I was reporting on the war in South Africa, I had jolly old Boers taking potshots at me on several occasions. The same thing happened in Cuba, and also in China during the Boxer affair. But those attempts were different. No, this had been a deliberate attempt to create bodily harm, and I was the target. Actually, I was equally surprised by my own reaction and the way my pistol had leapt into my hand as though it belonged there.

Well, I would not solve anything that night so, wedging a chair under the door to deter any potential intruder, I put my pistol under my pillow and went to sleep.

CHAPTER FOUR

In the morning, after shaving, ablutions and coffee, I set out to see if I could add to my general knowledge of the twenty-year-old shootout. My first stop was the town offices to see if their records had any inkling of what had transpired. I drew a blank. Not only did I receive bland negative replies to my queries, but I also experienced the distinct feeling that there was a lack of enthusiasm to delve into the past of Dogleg.

Although it was a trifle early, even for me, I dropped into the cantina where Pablo greeted me with a cheery smile and poured me a shot of tequila. Pulling my notebook from my pocket, I read through the poem for the umpteenth time, searching for I knew not what. Finally, I listed the names of all the characters described and decided to try and trace their individual fates. My list included Jenny Ling, Dapper Mike, the Bar 6 boys – how many? Names? The Mercantile – who owned the store, and also the bank? Who was Ezra? What eventually became of Bill Syke?

I resolved to ask Jane Bronson about some of the above when next I saw her but, in the meantime, I thought that perhaps I could put my reporter's investigative skills to work and see what I could do to enlarge the little data that I had gleaned to date.

First of all, who was 'Dapper Mike'? Well, we know that he was a gambler and presumably he dressed sharply, though possibly in a loud style. We also know that he was a central figure in the fracas that took place. Now gamblers had a tendency to move from town to town, either as the inclination took them, or because they had outlived their welcome in one specific berg. One other factor we can surmise about Dapper Mike is that he had probably been an experienced gun-hand, since he had survived until he encountered Bill Syke as dawn broke over the burning town.

I doubted whether I could find out any more about the gambler in Dogleg, but, since a telegraph line operated from the town to El Paso, I took a chance and sent a message to Joe Dolan, a newspaperman I knew in that city. I kept it brief: 'Joe. Seeking info. One 'Dapper Mike' Gambler/Gun-hand. Circa 1880-1890. Any data available.'

The telegraph clerk looked at me curiously as he read my message and sent it out over the wires, but I just put his reaction down to the fact that it was an unusual query. I asked around and found that I could cross one name off my list. Ezra, he of the mule corral, had retired from business six or seven years ago but shortly after doing so had fallen down a well in a drunken state and expired. Everyone to whom I spoke said that he had been one of the characters of the town. Garrulous, but with a heart of gold. Give you his shirt off of his back. Always good for a dollar – yet appeared to die penniless. A great pity.

I learned that the Bar 6 cattle ranch was still in business, about fifteen miles northwest of Dogleg, and resolved that the following morning, weather permitting, I would drive out that way and make a few enquiries. Meanwhile, I just circulated around Dogleg chatting to anyone about anything and trying to gather scraps of information about the history of the town. It was an uphill battle and got worse as the day progressed. Folks just tended to clam up directly the conversation drifted away from the weather or such mundane topics. It was very strange, as though I was encountering a wall of silence. The topic I was seeking had been probably the major event in the history of the town yet strangely nobody wanted to talk about it.

Eventually, at suppertime, I went to the Eatery and smiling at Jane took a vacant seat and waited to be served. She came up and took my order, a trifle nervously I thought but paid no more attention to it until, when bringing my coffee, she whispered, 'What have you been up to? The town's all riled up about you!'

I looked at her in bewilderment. 'I've just been asking historical questions about the town's early history. That's what reporters and correspondents do. They ask questions. Why would that get people all upset?'

'I understand that, Pete! And I believe you and I think that most reasonably minded people would be the same. But, somehow, someone has stirred up a number of the folks with the tale that you are here to make trouble for everyone, but not to worry! I'll keep telling them you're a good guy!'

Later, as she brought my dinner of steak, sawmill gravy and mashed potatoes, baked onion and biscuits, she said quietly, 'Come straight to the house tonight, rather than waiting in the street for me. Maybe there will be less for folks to talk about.'

I nodded and set to work demolishing the contents of the dinner plate which, followed by a slice of delicious apple pie, left me with a sense of satisfaction – at least gastronomically. After dinner I sat for a while savouring a third cup of coffee and left to check at the telegraph office. There was no reply from Joe Dolan but I wasn't surprised as it was early yet.

Later in the evening I made my way by a roundabout route to Jane Bronson's cottage. It was in darkness and I wondered whether I was too early. I tapped gently on the door and was relieved to hear a quiet voice enquire as to who was knocking.

'It's Pete Lomass, Jane!' I said, and waited.

I heard a bolt being withdrawn and moments later the door opened and I slipped in. Jane took my hand and guided me to a chair whilst she lit the oil lamp, keeping the wick low. I wondered why the drapes over the windows had been doubled by having additional cloth hung on them, so that no light would be seen outside.

I sought an answer. 'Jane! You seemed worried at the Eatery when I saw you earlier this evening and now I notice that you've gone to extra lengths to prevent anyone knowing that someone may be with you here. What has happened?'

'Pete, I'm scared! At first there were just vague suggestions that in Dogleg we just don't want strangers nosing around deliberately stirring up trouble. Then some of the remarks became a little bit more pointed and then finally I got this late in the afternoon, just before we started getting the dinner crowd.' And Jane handed me a folded sheet of paper, torn from a notepad.

I unfolded the note and read:

Jane, if you want to stay in business and out of trouble, keep your nose clean. Look what happened to Beth. Take a friendly warning!

I looked over at Jane. 'Did you see who delivered this rot?'

She shook her head. 'No, apparently it was just handed to one of the kitchen staff by a small boy who ran off immediately. So I've no idea as to who would write such a terrible thing!'

I tried to look at the issue rationally. 'Look Jane, whoever scribbled that rubbish must be one of the older residents of Dogleg, since more recent townsfolk may not know all the details of the rampage twenty years ago. We could almost certainly eliminate many people and see who's behind this threat.'

She looked at me gloomily and nodded. 'I know you're right Pete but. . .' she paused, twisting a lace handkerchief to ribbons as she was deciding whether to unburden herself with possibly more bad news. 'You'll recall that last night we briefly discussed the fact that old Ezra was no longer with us and the nature of his death. Well, I've been thinking about that. Shortly before the accident happened there was a great Tent Meeting in town, put on by a travelling preacher. He really put on quite a show and there were many people who took the Pledge and swore to stay away from demon drink. Ezra was one of them! Ezra had never really been a habitual drinker. The Pledge just cemented his belief that he didn't need booze to be happy. That's what he told me. Yet two weeks later he drowns in a well. Drunk! I have been wondering if he knew something about the night the town burnt and someone decided to shut him up – permanently!'

I looked at Jane gravely. 'From what you are telling me, the threat to you, Ezra's death, the shots last night, this is becoming truly serious, and I don't want you to be involved where you might be putting yourself in danger.'

'Oh, I'll be careful, Pete. But, as a stranger you are more likely to face outright hostility, so you must be extra careful!'

We talked a while longer about generalities and

then after Jane had extinguished the light I left, but not before I had given her a big hug, to which I'm glad to say she responded warmly.

CHAPTER FIVE

The next morning, after filling two canteens with fresh water, I wheeled the flivver out of its shed and drove off on the track that I had been told would take me to the Bar 6. It was a beautiful morning, fresh after an overnight shower. Everything was bright and crisp. The track was no worse than the road leading to Dogleg and my machine was behaving itself, with the engine purring along merrily.

We passed through rocky outcrops where the trail wound itself between huge boulders and I noticed that, imperceptibly, the ground was rising. In truth, the terrain was semi-desert with all the usual flora, now accompanied by a carpet of yellow flowers teased out by the overnight rain. All too soon the sun would be sending forth its searing heat and the flowers would shrivel and die.

As I drove along, my thoughts were continually flickering from one subject to another. What would I find, if anything, out at the Bar 6? Who shot at me and did that episode reflect the way the people of

Dogleg were beginning to treat me? In addition, I kept having another disturbing thought. What was my relationship with Jane Bronson? From the first moment that we had met I had sensed a certain feeling of comfort in her presence. There was a warmth in the way she smiled which called upon me to reciprocate. Which I found I was eager to do.

I had always considered myself as a typical hard-boiled newspaper correspondent, capable of experiencing all manner of situations, yet remaining objective and emotionally divorced from the drama around me. True, as a normal, healthy male animal, I had had brief sexual encounters in the past, but they had never amounted to anything. Somehow, in some strange way this was different.

While I thus ruminated we drove steadily on, with the trail dipping to cross a dry water-course which, I noted, would create a problem if one was faced with a flash flood, as so often happens with the sudden southern storms.

At last we arrived at a wire fence which, going off into the far distance, denoted the boundary of the Bar 6 ranch. Ownership was further reinforced by a wired five-bar gate, surmounted by an arch on which was inscribed 'Bar 6 Ranch – Josh Mortimer – owner.' The gate was closed with a common spring latch and, getting out to open said portal to drive in, I noticed yet another sign stating; 'Close the gate after you! Hey! This means you!'

I did as instructed, and drove on through rough grazing pasture dotted with healthy looking

Hereford cattle who ignored the growling machine that had appeared among them.

After a further fifteen minutes of driving, I brought the Ford to a halt outside a long, low ranch house that was impressive in its simplicity. In front there was a covered porch on which were a couple of rocking chairs and primitive side tables. The building was quite old, in that it was constructed with squared logs unlike the more common clapboard, and I noticed that the windows had shutters attached which, in more violent times, could be swung shut and locked to thwart enemy fire.

Off to the sides of the main house were a bunk house, barns, stables, a driving shed, and corrals containing a healthy number of cow ponies. All in all, the Bar 6 looked as though it was a prosperous enterprise.

As I walked up to the porch, the door opened revealing a small, daintily built lady, grey haired, well dressed, who smiled at me and said, 'Mister, I don't know what you're selling but it'd better be good for you to drive way out here.'

I tipped my hat to her and introduced myself, presenting my business card. She looked at the card, looked at me and looked at the card again. 'Well, I'm pleased to make your acquaintance Mr Lomass, but how can I help you?'

I described to her how I had found the poem and, having copied it down, felt compelled to seek out more about the story. I went on to tell how I came to Dogleg and, without going into details, indicated

that so far I hadn't made too much progress in deter-
mining exactly what had happened. I said that
perhaps if I spoke to Mr Mortimer, possibly he could
shed some light on the story since the cowboys had
been working for the Bar 6.

'I think, Mr Lomass, you'd better come inside out
of the heat.' She escorted me into an attractive living
room, vanished, and reappeared with a tall glass of
cool lemonade for me and one for herself. She asked
if I had a copy of the poem with me and I handed
over my notebook. Putting on spectacles she read the
handwritten copy through, put it down and read it
again, sighing as she did so.

'Mr Lomass, I think that I should tell you that
there is no Mr Mortimer! Josh died over twenty years
ago. I am Agnes Mortimer. I inherited the Bar 6 from
my father and Josh was one of my cowhands. He was
very handsome in a masculine way, brown wavy hair
and was one of the best hands on the ranch. We fell
madly in love and married, I, on my twenty-first birth-
day and Josh being in his mid-twenties. It was I who
suggested putting his name on the arch at the
entrance. He protested but I was adamant. I thought
it best to let the world believe there was a man in
charge. Silly really but, when young folks are in love
they do these things.

'That day Josh had had a good local sale of one
hundred cattle to a Scotsman who wanted to start a
ranch way to the west from here. He went into town,
to deposit the money in the Dogleg bank, and some
of the boys who had been paid that day persuaded

Josh to go along with them to Red Corcoran's saloon. Now, as I understand it, there was already bad blood between the Bar 6 boys and that wretched gambler Dapper Mike. He was suspected of some underhand dealing handling the cards, but nobody could ever prove anything. In addition, earlier he had made a pass at that young Jenny Ling and had been soundly rejected, whereas she was known to be more than friendly to quite a number of the young men of the area. Now, Mr Lomass, I know there were stories about her but I never judge a person until I know for sure, and nothing was ever proven about her activities.

'Mike had been buying drinks freely that night as the poem indicates. So when the trouble started he had plenty of back-up. Josh tried to get our boys to just leave the saloon but, with the liquor flowing, they were all determined to have a showdown. He went over to speak to Red – I believe to suggest that the bar be closed – and that's when the first shots were fired. I was later told that Red and Josh were both hit and killed at the same time and that neither man had drawn a gun.

'Their bodies were dragged out to the street as the saloon became an inferno and the next day a wagon brought poor Josh home to me. I buried him with his ma and pa on the small hill you can see over there,' indicating a hill surmounted with a grove of trees.

Agnes Mortimer fell silent, and her eyes stared into some far-off distant zone where brave young cowboys gaily flaunted their unique skills in riding, roping and handling six guns, as though the weapon was an extension of their own body. At length, she roused herself with a little shake and apologized for letting her memories lead her astray.

'I'm afraid that's all I can tell you about the Dogleg fire, Mr Lomass. I hope that my little story has been of some help.'

'It certainly has, Mrs Mortimer, and I'm sorry that I may have reawakened a dark chapter in your life, which you may well have wanted to remain closed. There are a couple of things. What were the names of the Bar 6 cowboys mentioned in the poem and what happened to them?'

'Certainly! Well, let me see. There was of course Josh, my husband; Bill Syke who took over as foreman after Josh married me; Ernie Martin, a good roper, and Cherokee – that was the only name we ever had. He used to break in all the wild mustangs we acquired. José Lopez was a very gentle man who played his guitar beautifully and the Kid, otherwise Patrick O'Rourke, a good cowhand with a terrible temper when roused. There were others, but those were the ones that went into Dogleg that awful day.

'I'm told that Patrick was one of the first to pull a gun that night. He was always practising his draw out back beyond the large corral and often said that he wished he had met that young outlaw in New Mexico, Billy the Kid. Patrick, at one time, even tried to persuade everyone that his nickname was "Kid O'Rourke".

'The last time Patrick was seen he was huddled on

the floor, dead, with his pistol dropped from his hand. He had been shot by one of the bartenders, armed with a sawed-off twelve-gauge Greener. Patrick had ignored a command to drop his gun and the barkeep let him have both barrels in the back. I understand that moments later the shooter fell, struck down by a stray bullet between the eyes. Mr Lomass, tell me! How can normal men turn into such beasts?'

I shook my head and commiserated with her. Having seen warfare in several parts of the world I was no longer surprised at the depths to which men could sink.

After a little while Mrs Mortimer continued, 'Patrick's body was never recovered and so was incinerated in the fire. As for the rest of the boys, well Bill Syke was badly shot up – it is a wonder that he survived. In addition to one in the left shoulder and one in the chest, a heavy slug, probably from a Sharps Buffalo gun, had slammed into his left hip shattering the hip bone and socket. It was a real mess. And, finally, he had a bullet in the lower leg. I forget which one.

'Bill refused to come back to the ranch. He maintained that he'd caused enough trouble. For a while he lived in a tent, until there was a building in town where he could rent a room. His argument was that the location was close to the doctor who was treating him. Then, directly he was capable of travelling, he upped and left. That was the last we saw of him.

'The other three boys came back to the ranch. They all had minor wounds but nothing too serious.

The Indian lad, Cherokee, stayed for a season and then drifted and we later learned that he had married a girl in what was then Indian territory, now Oklahoma. Ernie and José have stayed with us. Ernie is now the foreman and a very good top hand. I would be lost without him.

'José married a delightful Mexican girl and now we have a number of *bambinos* running around. José and Conchita live in a little cottage not far from the ranch house.'

I thanked Mrs Mortimer and prepared to take my leave. At that moment a rider rode up and dismounting, strode up to the front door and came straight in. He was a tall, rangy looking character, sunburned and wearing cattleman's gear; long-sleeved check shirt, blue jeans stuffed into long, scuffed brown boots, leather vest and yes, he was packing a pistol high up on the right side. He had removed his hat upon entering the building, revealing that he had but a scant head of hair. I would have guessed his age to be close on fifty.

His first remark was to Mrs Mortimer. 'Is this guy bothering you, boss?'

Agnes Mortimer hastened to explain who I was and the purpose of my visit. She assured Ernie that there had been no bother and that she was perfectly safe. She then gave Ernie an account of our conversation and concluded by suggesting that perhaps Ernie might have some additional information.

Ernie and I shook hands and he scratched his sparse head of hair. 'Wal, Pete,' he said, 'I don't know as how I can add anything to what Mizz Mortimer told you. Bill Syke and I wus always good pals and I just couldn't figure out why he took off jus' like that. It's as though he jus' dropped off the edge of the world. I tell you what though. This is not a clue, just a hunch on my part. Before the fracas at Red's saloon, sometimes we'd just sit in the evening outside the bunkhouse, smoking and yarning. Day dreamin' I guess you'd call it. Bill used to often say that he'd like to go down into Old Mexico. He said that he liked the people, their lifestyle and their generosity towards strangers. By the way, Bill was not wantin' a penny or two. Apart from the very odd spree he'd socked his money away carefully and could have retired anytime. That's all I can add, sorry.'

I went out to the car accompanied by Ernie and Mrs Mortimer and, after thanking them profusely for their assistance, headed back towards Dogleg. It was late afternoon when I left the ranch and I wanted to make the journey before nightfall since, being this far south, I knew that there would be no long period of twilight. One moment the sun would be a huge fiery ball balanced on the rim of the horizon, and in the next two or three minutes it would be gone, leaving the world in darkness.

CHAPTER SIX

We were about halfway to Dogleg, and I was thinking that I should light the acetylene headlamps before darkness descended when, as the car lurched to the left and the wheel sank into a pothole, the windshield shattered, spraying glass fragments around as the sound of a shot echoed among the surrounding hills.

I yanked violently on the steering wheel pulling the car off the track and into the midst of a number of yucca plants, which furnished a certain amount of camouflage, and immediately dived from the seat to the ground as a second shot smashed into the bodywork of the car.

My face was stinging from a number of small cuts caused by the bullet that had hit the windshield but, fortunately, my eyes were protected by my driving goggles. Having mopped rather ineffectually at my cuts with a grubby handkerchief, I hunkered down by the side of the car and considered my next move.

Point number one: those shots were no accident.

The first, theoretically, could have been, but the second one indicated that the shooting had been deliberate. As if to verify my train of thought a third round came winging amid the yuccas, prompting me to crawl several yards to my right to a slight depression that provided me with an element of cover.

Point number two: Lomass, what are you going to do about it? Or more correctly, what could I do about it? Well, I could wait the night out hoping that the unknown shooter would give up and depart, or I could endeavour to figure out where he was and possibly try to take some form of offensive action of my own.

I found myself wishing that I had a long gun handy, one of the new Government Springfields would be extremely useful right now. But I didn't have one so it was no good crying for the moon! What I did have was my 1878 Colt with one good feature. Despite the fact that the barrel had been reduced to six inches with the military model such as mine, with sufficient elevation one could drop a bullet accurately as far as 100 feet.

There was another shot in the general direction of the car and I figured that the shooter was firing without knowing exactly where I was hiding, but hoping that the shooting would cause me to come into the open where he could finish the game.

Well, two could play that hand. I had noticed where his last shot came from. The muzzle flash told me he was in a low jumble of rocks to the west of the track and the quarter moon, just rising, showed a shadowy image of his location. I aimed, with my Colt held steady in both hands, and waited for his next shot.

It came and as the noise echoed again and again, I triggered three shots fast. The first directly at the muzzle flash, the second and third a little to either side. Then I waited and while doing so reloaded my pistol. All was silent and there were no more shots fired.

The night passed slowly and got darned cold in the early hours of the morning. Finally, there was a streak of light along the eastern horizon heralding the dawn of another day. Still no movement from the rocks. Finding a long stick I placed my hat on it and waved it to and fro to attract attention. Still no response. Finally, on my belly, I crawled forward at an angle to his position and at length rose and ran crouching, with my pistol extended in the right hand, approaching his place of concealment from the side. I need not have bothered. My opponent was no longer a problem. One of my three shots had struck him squarely on the temple and penetrating the skull had proved to be fatal. A single-shot Springfield trapdoor rifle of 45/70 calibre was tucked partially under the body. The rifle was very familiar to me, having seen plenty of them in Cuba during our war with the Spanish.

After picking up a couple of empty shell cases as evidence, I returned to my poor old Ford and after dint of effort got it clear of the yuccas and back on the track. Would it start? It did and, after cleaning

48

away some of the glass fragments, I drove back into Dogleg, cursing the lack of my windshield.

My first stop was the county sheriff's office where, after pounding on the door, I aroused that worthy from his slumbers. He was not happy! However, after hearing my story, and consuming two mugs of coffee and even generously providing one for me, he agreed to drive out with me to the site of the ambush.

When we reached the spot, to my amazement the body had gone, as had the rifle. At first the sheriff thought that I was indulging in some sort of prank, but sobered up when I pointed out the blackened blood on the rocks, the other shell cases, which coincided with the two I had produced in his office, and, above all, the tracks of a heavy vehicle which had drawn up close to the rocks.

We returned to Dogleg and to his office. The sheriff, George Duval, a political appointee, was in a quandary. Being county sheriff meant that his jurisdiction was limited to areas outside the city limits of the various communities but this crime (if there was one), though occurring in the countryside, undoubtedly had its origin in Dogleg. He decided at length to have a discussion with Al Watson, the town marshal, and see if between them they might be able to gather more information.

CHAPTER SEVEN

Meanwhile I was free to go about my business, which I did, heading first to my room where I shaved and had a good strip-down wash. Looking at myself in the mirror, I realized that the night's adventure had not improved my appearance. A rugged, tanned face, surmounted by a mop of brown curly hair, was now speckled with tiny cuts from the broken windshield! I dressed, and my next task was to locate a mechanic or someone who could replace my shattered wind-shield. In this I was unlucky. The twentieth century hadn't reached Dogleg yet. My third task was to head for the Eatery where I looked forward to having the best breakfast in the house.

The place wasn't too busy so I had no trouble obtaining a table to myself. Jane saw me, hurried over and stopped short when she saw my face, which – despite my attentions back in my bedroom – still looked as if I had been in a fight or had encountered a very angry cat.

'Pete!' she whispered. 'What on earth happened

to you? You look awful!'

'Don't worry Jane! It's nothing really. Just had a little bit of an accident while coming back from the Bar 6. I had a broken windshield and some splinters of glass hit me. It'll look much better tomorrow.'

Jane stood there, hands on her hips, staring down at me. 'I don't know what we're going to do with you, Pete! I guess that the truth is you need someone to look after you.'

Having said that she turned bright red as I replied, 'Why? Are you looking for a job?' At which remark Jane scurried away muttering something about bringing coffee. Without my placing an order I found myself confronted with the biggest breakfast in the house, with three eggs, ham, bacon, a medium-sized steak and a large quantity of golden home fries together with hot biscuits. By the time I had done full justice to that meal, washed down with several cups of coffee I might add, I was ready to take on the world.

I went to pay my score and was told it was on the house. A gift from Miss Bronson, who had slipped out to go to the bank. Obviously, Jane did not want to be interrogated regarding her last remark.

Since Jane was not around to be brought up to date, I made my way to the telegraph office and checked with the duty clerk. 'Lomass is the name. Pete Lomass. Any messages for me?'

He rummaged among the pigeon holes and at length produced a 'flimsy' and, consulting his incoming book, marked a place for me to sign as a receipt for the message. Having collected a dollar, he

51

finally handed it over. I opened the folded flimsy and read: *Dapper Mike; born 1860 Michael Carstairs. Place of Birth, New York City. All for now. Joe Dolan.*

I was in a quandary. The only person with whom I could share my problems was Jane Bronson and there were two reasons why I couldn't do so. First of all I didn't want to involve her in what was apparently becoming a dangerous situation and, secondly, she had wisely appeared to limit our association. Until I could have a long chat with Jane I could do no more in Dogleg, unless either the town marshal or the county sheriff uncovered any further information.

I had been informed that the closest place where I could get the windshield replaced was a workshop in El Paso and, being up against the proverbial brick wall in Dogleg, I decided to make the journey and get my sad-looking Ford repaired. So, having settled my account for the room and written a brief note for Jane to explain why I was leaving and intimating that I would be returning shortly, I headed westward.

The journey was uneventful. The highway, a pothole-filled track, was identical to all the others in rural Texas and the Ford performed valiantly, chugging along as we lurched and swayed towards El Paso. I didn't know too much about the place except that it was located right on the Rio Grande and faced the Mexican city of Ciudad Juarez across the river. Apparently, El Paso had been nicknamed the 'Six shooter capital' because of the degree of lawlessness that went on there and I had been advised to keep one hand on my wallet and the other on my pistol grip whilst there.

I entered the city and, after making cautious enquiries, located a hardware store that was also the dealership for Ford automobiles. From there I was directed to a workshop, which was doing repairs on a number of these newfangled modes of transportation. The owner and chief mechanic, in fact the only one, assured me that he could replace the windshield, although it might take a few days as he'd have to get the part shipped to El Paso by rail.

Reluctantly, I told him to go ahead and order the part and, taking my grip, I went forth to seek accommodation for the next few days. During the ten-minute walk to the Sunrise Hotel I was accosted by several young, and not so young, ladies of doubtful virtue, all of whom wanted to give me the best time of my life. Two gentlemen offered their services as city guides, prepared to show me the best saloons, the best gambling establishments and the best houses, where still more young ladies of every colour were longing to satisfy my every desire, and, finally, a bewhiskered old codger sidled up and, muttering that he'd struck it rich, offered to share his good fortune with me for just a small investment.

Reaching the hotel I booked a room on the second floor and, after a quick wash and shave, decided to contact Joe Dolan. The hotel had a telephone and, phoning the exchange, I was put through to the *El Paso Herald* for whom Joe had been working for quite a few years. Joe wasn't available but

I left a message for him to contact me as soon as he returned to his desk.

Meanwhile, I consoled myself at the hotel bar and made friends with Harry the barman. He turned out to be quite a character, having been born and raised in El Paso and, since he was now in his late sixties, and having served as a barman all over the city, he had an encyclopaedic knowledge of the events that had made the area notorious. In fact, Harry assured me that he had been working in the Acme Saloon bar on the night of August 19th 1895 when Constable John Selman Sr appeared, and put two bullets into the head of one of the most vicious gunmen known in the West, John Wesley Hardin.

Curiously, two years later to the day, Harry had been working at another drinking establishment, the Wigwam, when that same John Selman was shot and mortally wounded in a back alley behind the saloon by one George Scarborough.

'I tell you, Mr Lomass, this city ain't a patch on what it was like before the turn of the century. True, there's plenty of vice still around, and the bunco artists are still at work as no doubt you have found out, but in those days, most of these characters daresn't have operated here. There was gun play on the streets practically every day and night. Yes, I will have a small one with you. Thank you kindly!' and Harry deftly poured himself a shot of rye whiskey while he simultaneously performed the time-honoured practice of wiping the surface of the bar-top with a white cloth clutched in his left hand.

On pure speculation, I posed a question to my garrulous friend. 'Harry! In all your years working in saloons around the city did you ever come across a gambler known as Dapper Mike, or maybe Mike Carstairs? May have come from New York?'

'How old would this galoot have been, Mr Lomass?'

'Well Harry, I don't really know but let's make a guess. Say twenty years ago. I'm thinking that he'd have been probably just under or just over thirty years of age.'

'Twenty years ago you say! Hmm! So, we're talking about 1888 to say 1890. Lemme see now!'

Harry's features developed a ferocious scowl as he cast his mind back through the years. I waited patiently, not wishing to talk and thereby disturb his train of thought. Several minutes passed in silence and, finally, Harry adopted a triumphant air as he muttered to himself.

'Gotcha! I seem to recall a person who possibly would have fitted the description you gave. About twenty-five years ago a Smart Alec gambler was active in El Paso. He was young, say about mid to late twenties. Fancy dresser. But then most gamblers tended to be like that in those days. He talked kinda funny. Could've bin a Noo York accent. He fancied himself as a gunfighter, though he wouldn't have stood a chance against a man like Bill Hickok. No, this galoot perforated a pilgrim who claimed that he'd been cheated. The pilgrim didn't die but the boys suggested that Noo York seek greener fields. I can't remember his name but he was a flashy dresser.

'Now, here's the interesting thing about this guy we're discussing. About eighteen years ago he came back. Looked as though he'd been on the losing end of a gunfight. He limped. Had a bad cough and his right hand was twisted up like a claw. Certainly no good for shuffling cards. He came in here. Had a couple of drinks at the bar. Very quiet like. Said he was looking for a friend who was travelling with a young girl. Asked me to let him know if I ever heard any news of the couple.' Harry dipped his hand under the bar, opened a drawer and came up with a dirty, time-worn business card. 'He left this with me.'

I took the card and noted the inscription 'Miles Carson. Real Estate. General Delivery. Denver, Co.' Miles Carson. Michael Carstairs. An interesting similarity!

'Mr Lomass, a strange thing happened shortly after Carson left. One morning as I was preparing the bar for the daily rush, two people came into the saloon and specifically asked for me. One was a tall, lean, weather-beaten man who had cowboy written all over him. I figured that he may have been piled up by a bronc at some time as he was sure crippled up, walking on crutches with one leg just swinging loose from the hip. He was accompanied by a dainty young woman, neatly dressed, as pretty as a picture. She maybe was foreign in some way, but I couldn't quite figure out the relationship between her and the busted-up cowboy.

'He spoke to me and came straight to the point.

"Mr Chambers,"' Harry indicated that that was his surname, to be employed on formal occasions, "Mr Chambers, I understand that a certain tin-horn gambler has been in here and would like to be informed when I was in the vicinity. For certain reasons I do not desire to meet Mike Carstairs, or whatever he chooses to call himself now. I'm certainly not scared of him, but I have been persuaded," and here he looked down at his little companion, "that discretion is the better part of valour! Therefore, it would be deeply appreciated if our short visit to El Paso remains a private affair."

'Now, Mr Lomass, when Carson had asked me to be on the lookout for the two people he described I, thinking he was merely wanting to meet old friends, had certainly spread the word across the city. After meeting the couple I realized that Carson's desire was not beneficial, but more likely one of revenge or some other ulterior motive, and so I have never contacted him. In fact, I assured the couple – she addressed him as Bill while he called her Angel – that their visit to El Paso would remain a secret as far as I was concerned. With that they left, and I've never seen hide nor hair of them since that day. All I know is that they headed south into Mexico.'

The information that Harry had imparted was certainly interesting. It would appear that whoever wrote the poem about the shootout at Dogleg had either been misinformed or had deliberately indicated that neither Bill Syke nor Dapper Mike were likely to have survived the duel in Ezra's corral, yet in the same time frame we have two people, both of whom are recovering from grave injuries, turn up in El Paso where one is eager to continue the feud, while the other is obviously not.

What should be my next step, I pondered. Joe Dolan had still not appeared and it seemed that most of the information that he could have provided had been furnished by Harry the barman. I had been told that the repairs to my Ford would probably take anywhere up to two weeks, during which time I'd have to kick up my heels in El Paso, which was hardly a pleasing prospect. A thought struck me; 'Harry, do you by any chance know where Crippled Bill and the girl were heading when they crossed over into Mexico?'

'I don't rightly know, Mr Lomass, but Big Bill spoke to the girl and included the word Chihuahua, so it's possible that that was their destination – the city I mean, not the state.'

It was a very slim lead with which to head into another country but, over the years as a reporter, I had followed far less information in the hopes of obtaining a scoop for my newspaper. I had the time, and money was no problem. Therefore, I decided to travel south and see if I could pick up a trail now about twenty years old.

Harry proved to be an invaluable assistant being very familiar with Ciudad Juarez and he quickly drew me a sketch map showing the best way to get from the bridge over the Rio Grande to the railroad station, where I could book passage to Chihuahua City. Being fairly conversant with Spanish, especially

58

after my time in Cuba, I was confident that I could make myself understood south of the border.

As Harry and I were having a final discussion, there was an interruption. A tall man clad in the uniform of the El Paso police force entered the saloon and came straight up to me. He nodded to Harry and turning to me enquired, 'Your name Lomass, sir?' I acknowledged that that was my name and he continued, 'We understand that you had an appointment to meet a certain Joséph Dolan in this saloon today – time unspecified. Is that so?'

Again I admitted that his information was correct and then gave a query of my own. 'Look, officer, what is this all about? I'm a newspaper reporter myself and Joe was doing a little job for me, ferreting out information for a story I'm working on. Now, sir! What gives?'

'Well, Mr Lomass, your Joe Dolan won't be doing any work for you in the future. He was found floating in the river this morning with a knife between his shoulder blades. He was last seen the previous night at about ten-thirty, leaving the offices of the *Herald*. He'd just received a telephone call that got him mighty agitated and he jumped up and left immediately. Would you know anything about that?'

I shook my head in bewilderment. Joe, dead! Murdered! I explained that the previous evening I had spent the whole time chatting to Harry and to a couple of the regular patrons of the saloon, all of which could be easily verified. I further indicated that in fact I hadn't seen Joe Dolan for several years and had been conducting my business with him by telegraph, which could be easily checked. The officer assured me that they had already determined that my story was watertight and that I was never a suspect. As usual the police were merely following every lead. And with that, he gave me a half salute and left.

CHAPTER EIGHT

I left and headed for the bridge to take me into Mexico. There were no border guards in those days and nobody was interested in what I was taking into the country. As I was walking to the railroad station and beating off the dozens of small Mexicanos offering to carry my grip; clean my shoes; show me a good barber; and even suggesting that I might like to inspect their older sister for my pleasure, I pondered over the murder of Joe Dolan. Obviously, the shots at Jane's cottage in Dogleg, the ambush set for me as I returned from the Bar 6 and Joe's murder could be connected. But why? And again, equally, they could be totally separate incidents.

I found the station. Paid for a return ticket first class to Chihuahua City and got a seat in *de primera clase* (the first class) car. The whole car was clean and the seats comfortable and gradually other passengers arrived as the time of departure drew close. Most of my fellow travellers were Mexicans of both sexes and were probably, I assumed, of the upper class as the poorer people could not have afforded first class fare.

In addition, there were two fellow Americans and also three Germans, engineers by their conversation, and arrogant in the way they addressed the car attendant as though he was something below them. He, in return, remained icily polite, but I saw his face as he turned away from them and it was not a pretty sight.

The countryside through which we passed was one of contrasts. Areas of arid semi-desert, with typical cacti and other plants capable of survival with limited water, were interspersed with areas where peons dwelt and attempted to scratch a living from the soil. Their dwellings tended to be monotonously uniform, consisting of once-white adobe one-room houses in which entire families eked out an existence.

Very occasionally, the train passed by a large hacienda surrounded by well-cultivated and irrigated fields that were being tended by white-garbed peons, supervised by mounted overseers. The contrast between rich and poor was very obvious, compared to the standards of living in the United States of America.

The train travelled from the flat lowlands into hilly territory where the inclines became apparent as the locomotive laboured to draw its burden up through a series of defiles. The speed of the train slowed and then came to a sudden halt as the engineer reduced the steam pressure. Simultaneously, the door at the end of the car burst open and in poured a number of

Mexicans dressed as peons, with large straw sombreros but literally bristling with weapons.

By words and gestures common worldwide, all the passengers were herded out and lined up along the side of the track, guarded by several dozen swarthy brigands continually shouting and waving their firearms and machetes in our faces.

The uproar ceased with the arrival of a heavily built man mounted upon a beautiful white horse. The rider was dressed with garb similar to his followers with the addition of a coloured poncho draped across his broad shoulders and he displayed an air of authority.

Dismounting, he walked along the line of passengers staring fiercely at some and smiling at others – mostly at females I should add. He came to me and I looked him squarely in the eye, noting the pock marks on his face and the drooping, unkempt moustache. He grunted and walked on.

Having surveyed his prisoners once, Francisco as his men addressed him (though the world would one day know him as Pancho Villa) drew a wicked-looking Mauser semi-automatic pistol (of the type carried by my fellow correspondent Winston Churchill in South Africa) and brandishing it, stalked back and forth along the line.

I sensed that he was working himself up into a killing mood and I was not mistaken. Coming opposite the three Germans he turned to face them and waving his pistol said something to the effect that his gun was a good German whereas they were bad

Germans. So saying he fired once, twice and yet again.

His aim was accurate. All three men were driven back by the close range shots that hammered into them and, lifeless, they slumped to the ground. Pleased with his handiwork, he chose yet another victim. Being informed that one of the well-dressed Mexicans was the *Alcalde*, that is the mayor of a small community, he proceeded to verbally abuse the poor fellow who, terrified, fell to his knees in supplication.

It was of no avail. His tormentor appeared to listen earnestly to the mayor's pleas, nodding his head wisely as if in agreement, and suddenly raised his pistol and shot the man between the eyes before his wife and three small children. The air was rent with the shrieks and wails of the distraught widow and her offspring and continued until a roar of '*Silencio*' prompted them to reduce their grief to a continuous silent sobbing. Villa meanwhile was intent on searching out further victims.

He came up to me and stared long and hard into my face. I tried my hardest to remain unconcerned and stared back at him. Finally, he spoke.

'You, Gringo! What you do?' By which fractured English I gathered that he wished to know what I did for a living.

'I am a correspondent. I write for American newspapers.'

Villa tried to wrap his tongue around the word 'correspondent'. He frowned. 'This word correspond . . . how you say it? What is it you do?'

'Well, I write stories about people and places and the things that people are doing. These are then put in the newspapers and are read by millions of other people. That is how people in one part of the world learn what is happening in other places.'

'What do they call you, Señor writer?'

'My family name is Lomass. My first name is Peter, but my friends call me Pete.'

'Ah, Peter. You mean Pedro, *sî*?' Villa smiled at me and I began to have high hopes of seeing yet another day.

'So, Pedro, you will write a story about me and my men and this will be told to all Americanos?'

The last thing that I wanted was to become the mouthpiece for a bunch of Mexican *banditos* but since I possessed a very natural desire to remain alive, I nodded and then posed a question. 'I will write an article about you but I must have a typewriter. Do you have one?'

He looked at me in bewilderment. The word meant nothing to him and I elaborated, 'A machine that prints letters so I can make them into words.'

He called over one of his men and they chatted away in voluble Spanish before his henchman leapt upon his horse and rode off at a gallop.

Meanwhile, the remainder of the gang were engaged in looting the train of any merchandise being shipped, and also the personal possessions of the passengers. Strangely, my grip was returned to me intact, even though my Colt and holster were lying on top of the change of clothing and my shaving kit.

The passengers were then permitted to re-board the train and the engineer was motioned to continue with the journey. I was left standing by myself beside the rails along with the four corpses – the Mexican mayor and the three no-longer-arrogant Germans.

Villa appeared astride his white horse and leading another saddled mount. 'Come, we go to my camp.'

I went to pick up my grip and he quickly ordered one of the band to bring the 'gringo's *maleta* and don't lose it or you will be very sorry'. The *peon* so ordered hurried to pick up my grip, assuring me that all would be safe in his care.

I mounted awkwardly and, since I had not been on a horse for a couple of years, was ill at ease for quite a while as we climbed higher into the mountains along a little-used trail that clung to the side of a precipice. To my left was the rocky face of the mountain; to my right the ground fell away into the unplumbed depths of the valley below.

To add to my miseries the horse did not like me. Most probably he didn't like any human being but, even on this narrow and precarious trail where one false step could send both steed and rider plunging to their deaths, he still kept twisting his head round in an attempt to bite me with his big yellow teeth.

At last my purgatory was over as we descended into a hidden valley where Pancho Villa had his headquarters. The ground was dotted with makeshift dwellings, mostly consisting of pieces of canvas draped over a couple of sticks. There were three or four military-style tents, no doubt borrowed from the Mexican army, and I was allotted part of one of these palatial abodes. My grip appeared and with the addition of a rather smelly blanket, it was considered that I had all the comforts of home.

Villa approached my tent. 'Pedro, come! We eat then we talk!' He led me to a place where food was being served by several female camp followers. I could not help noticing that nearly all of them were young and rather comely by Mexican standards.

The meal was adequate, by my own North American standards, consisting of pinto beans in a sauce heavily laced with chilli pepper and a few pieces of unidentified meat, thus making the dish a chilli con carne. There were also beans from an earlier meal, which had been somehow refried and therefore given new life. These were accompanied by flapjack-like pancakes, which the Mexicans described as *tortillas*. The object was to pile beans, or whatever else the diner had available, onto their flapjack and then roll it up like a huge cigar and convey it thus to the mouth.

When I had been reporting on the conflict in Cuba I had been warned to avoid the native foodstuffs and stick to the US military rations to which we correspondents were entitled. I had done so and, therefore, the meal in Villa's camp was my first introduction to a purely Mexican diet, washed down with several mugs of dubious-looking coffee. I hoped that I would survive until morning!

After the meal was over Pancho took me to one

side and said, 'Now we talk! I will tell you of my life and you will write it on the machine that makes words.'

I got out my notepad and listened while Pancho Villa talked hour after hour of his life story. From time to time I wrote down words or phrases that revealed some fresh aspect of the man's character and the things in which he believed.

Briefly, born in 1878 he had grown up the son of a sharecropper on a wealthy hacienda where the gulf between the peons and the landowners was always apparent. The vast majority of the *peons* were bound to the land by debt incurred by their generation or the previous one. Villa had received a limited education at the village school, but was barely literate.

In his teens he ran foul of the law. He apparently killed a man who had raped his sister and was hunted by the *Rurales*, the nationwide police force organized by the Mexican dictator, Porfirio Díaz. It would seem that Villa had gradually been developing a social conscience because, in our talks, he repeatedly indicated that he and his men would gladly join in a revolution to help right some of the wrongs with which Mexico was afflicted.

This explained some of his actions at the earlier rail holdup. The mayor that he had shot had been the instigator of a reign of terror in the area that he administered and, in Villa's eyes, his death was a justifiable execution. Likewise, the three Germans were actually army officers travelling in mufti while in Mexico, but they were engaged in training the

Mexican army in some of the more modern methods of warfare. Therefore, they represented a threat to any potential revolution.

CHAPTER NINE

I went to sleep that night lulled by the haunting melody of 'La Paloma', played by a one-eyed swarthy bandit on a guitar amid mental images of peons running amok led by a larger-than-life Pancho Villa.

The following morning I was hardly awake when he entered my tent with a loud greeting of, '*Buenos dias* Pedro! Get up! Come and see what a beautiful word-making machine I have got for you. Come!'

I stumbled out, shivering in the raw mountain air, and still gathering my wits together as I followed Villa to his headquarters tent, a rather tattered affair, formerly the property of some bygone circus.

Bidding me enter he stood staring into a corner, as proud of his new possession as a father showing off his new son and heir. 'What do you think of this, Pedro? Is it not magnificent?'

I looked closely. There, on an old battered school desk, was a decrepit, early model Oliver typewriter. I gulped. The steel carriage, commonly baked a uniform matte black, had been reduced to a speck-led grey through years of use and misuse. Examining this 'magnificent' machine with a professional eye I noted the following; the key top had one letter missing. It happened to be the letter A, which is one of the most commonly used! The platen, rather than being a smooth roller, looked as though it had been savaged by a ferocious dog with the surface hacked and pecked along its length. The ribbon responsible for transmitting the letters onto paper looked so worn that a casual eye would have immediately con-signed it to a garbage can. The platen gear had one tooth broken off and the carriage return lever was bent and flopped alarmingly when called upon to function in its normal manner.

Villa stood by awaiting my evaluation of his machine. I shrugged my shoulders with an attempt at humour. 'Well, Pancho, it's not quite what I'm used to but perhaps I can make it work, but where is the paper upon which I am to write the story of all your adventures?'

Villa slapped one hand into the other as he real-ized the obvious.

'Martinez, you idiot! Did you not get any paper when you went to seek out a typing machine for Pedro?'

Martinez looked at Villa in dismay, possibly ashamed at having not carried out his assignment efficiently, but more probably scared of the retribu-tion that might follow his error. 'I will go this instant, my chief, and will be back before you can realize that

71

I've been away.'

I held up my right hand. 'Wait Martinez!' I inserted a page torn from my notebook and attempted to type a sentence or two. The keys hit the paper, even the letter A, not withstanding the fact that I had to pause each time that letter was used to avoid being speared by the end of the letter arm, but the words did not appear – the dried-out ribbon was absolutely useless!

I turned to Villa. 'Look, Pancho! You can see that this machine must have a new ribbon to transmit the letters onto paper. Martinez must go to a store and get one.' I quickly wrote down the model number of the Oliver and the number of the ribbon barely discernible on the end of the spool. 'Martinez, this is what you must ask for in a store that sells similar machines.'

Martinez left on his quest for typewriter ribbon and paper and I set myself the task of attempting to refurbish that poor old Oliver. I borrowed a small screwdriver from Villa's armourer, the rather grand title for the handyman who repaired any firearms capable of restoration, in addition to his other duties around the camp.

With the screwdriver I tightened all screws that retained any thread and cleaned and oiled all parts that I thought required attention. While so engaged, I thought about the fact that Martinez indicated that he would be back shortly which, if true, would indicate that Villa had deliberately brought me to the camp by a long, roundabout route, first to confuse me and secondly, I think, to see how I reacted when faced with such a dangerous situation.

My ministrations appeared to have some success. The typewriter performed reasonably well and with the addition of a duplicate letter A, a small wooden one mounted on the end of the arm, I felt confident that with a new tape I would be able to produce something.

Meanwhile, I boldly told Pancho Villa that it was imperative that I get to Chihuahua City as soon as possible.

'Why for you go to Chihuahua, Pedro?' he queried.

I explained that I was looking for a man, an Americano who might be living there. He wanted to know what sort of a man I was seeking and so I told him. 'This Americano he is crippled as far as I know. He was badly shot up in a gunfight about twenty years ago.'

Villa looked at me rather strangely. 'What for you look for this man, Pedro? You would shoot him, *sí*?'

I shook my head vehemently. 'No, no! I don't wish him any harm. I just want to talk with him about the shootout in which he was badly injured.'

He nodded and at that moment there were shots as a fight broke out elsewhere in the camp. Villa jumped to his feet. '*Madre de Dios*!' he declared. 'If they want to fight why don't they take on the *Rurales*, not try to kill each other,' and he hurried from the tent. I followed more cautiously. I had no desire to be the victim of a stray bullet.

Across the other side of the campsite two men faced each other in anger, screaming vile epithets back and forth, each waiting for the other to make the next move. One had blood dripping down the side of his neck from a shot that had nicked his left ear, while the other held a clenched hand from which blood trickled to irrigate the ground. Their pistols were currently pointing at the ground rather than each other, which was a hopeful sign. I then saw an example of how Pancho Villa dispensed justice.

Villa surveyed each man and, pulling his Mauser, fired two shots rapidly into the air at the same time calling for silence. 'Now you *caballeros*, you want to fight. H'OK, so you will fight as gentlemen.'

He ordered them to stand five or six paces apart with their pistols held waist-high, aiming at each other, thus they would be shooting at point blank range. 'Are you ready? Now, when I give the word you will fire at each other.'

The two reluctant duelists looked aghast at their prospects of surviving such a fight and both lowered their pistols clear of their opponent. Then the words came tumbling out. They did not want to fight. It was all in the heat of an argument. If Villa could solve the dispute they would become once more the best of friends, they explained. There was a certain girl, Conchita by name. They were both passionately in love with her and she had declared her love for both of them, but could not decide who should be her true love.

Villa laughed. 'You are a pair of dolts! You are

friends. Friends share. One of you will have Conchita for one week and the other will have her for the following seven days. You will both decide, by cutting cards, who has the first week. High card wins.' Villa turned and motioning me to follow, left the two frustrated lovers to work out the new regulations governing their affections.

Shortly after, Martinez rode into the hideout, triumphant that he had been successful in both of his quests. He had somewhere managed to locate a spool of typewriter ribbon that fitted the Oliver and, from the same source, had obtained a packet of 8½ by 11 inch typing paper. Installing the fresh ribbon and loading a sheet of paper in place, with fingers crossed, I commenced to try and create sense out of the notes that I had taken while Villa had talked earlier.

It was an uphill task! That damned old rickety Oliver seemed determined to thwart me at every mechanical action it performed. Every time I pressed down upon a key it was with a sense of relief that the arm rose to deliver the required symbol on the white paper. The machine grunted and groaned at every movement, as though it was protesting at being forced into service after being retired for so long.

The one good thing was the fact that Villa kept out of my work area as I laboured to complete the task he had set me. For which I was extremely grateful, as there were many moments when my temper was close to boiling point as I struggled with that recalcitrant machine of the devil.

At length I was finished and, having glanced through my draft, called Pancho to my 'office' and read it to him. He was overjoyed. 'Pedro, you have put down my thoughts exactly as I told them to you. Now how do we get this into a newspaper?'

I explained that the article would have to be sent with my covering letter to the newspaper for which I worked and the editor would then decide when it would be published. That part of the process, I explained carefully, was completely out of my hands.

'All we can do is get my draft in the mail and wait until it is published. I've done what you asked me to, Pancho. Now I must be on my way to Chihuahua City to try and find him that I seek.'

He looked at me and grinned, shaking his head slowly from side to side and my heart sank. What fresh task would he have me perform before I could continue with my own life? Then he spoke and I was startled by his words.

'Pedro, my friend. You do not need to go as far as Chihuahua City. I know the man that you have been seeking. I think it is Señor Bill. He is a very good man and you can get to his place tomorrow. I myself, Pancho Villa, will take you. But now we must celebrate. You have done what I asked of you and I am sad that you are leaving. But, Pancho always keeps his word, as you have kept yours. Come Pedro, we must eat and drink to your departure!'

CHAPTER TEN

The following morning, with head throbbing from the effect of the festivities the previous evening, Pancho Villa, Martinez and I rode down out of the mountains into a long valley in the far distance of which could be seen the outline of a fair-sized village.

I remarked rather sarcastically to Pancho that it was a much easier ride than the one to which he had subjected me to when going to his camp. He laughed and replied with an air of embarrassment, 'Ah, Pedro! I had to test you to see if you were truly a man! You passed!'

I must say I was a trifle pleased with myself that I had met with his approval since, despite the fact that he was but a semi-literate bandit, Pancho Villa's approbation of one's character indicated that one had indeed emerged triumphant from a stern test.

We drew nearer to the village which I learned was known as Aqua Nuova, presumably because of the existence of an ever-flowing well of the life-giving fluid. The settlement had obviously developed around the well, which was located in the centre of the village square. On one side was a small white-washed church, on the other side a cantina flanked by a small general store catering to the villagers' simple needs and another building from which came the sound of children singing. My guess that this latter building was the village school proved to be correct, and all around the square and beyond were the whitewashed adobe dwellings of the peons who worked the surrounding fields.

We rode across the square and dismounted in front of the store. Martinez stayed with the horses as Pancho and I entered the building, passing from the sharp glare of a midday sun into the welcome gloom of the interior. I paused, giving my eyes time to adjust to the reduced light and began to discern the features of the store's interior.

I was in a large room divided into two halves by a counter that ran across from wall to wall. On my side there were three or four small tables with chairs where apparently patrons could sit and consume a meal or merely exchange the news of the day. Beyond the counter were shelves stacked high with the products that the villagers could not provide themselves. These included clothing and bolts of white cloth, needles and types of thread, ribbons, an array of metal tools and utensils, and a variety of canned goods.

All were in the care of a large well-built grey-haired man who sat on a stool beyond the counter, engrossed in an American newspaper of recent vintage. He looked up. '*Buenos dias, Señores*!' and then recognizing Pancho continued, 'Ah, Francisco my friend, it is so good to see you!' The use of Pancho's baptismal name was apparently for the benefit of two *Rurales* sitting in a corner playing a game of checkers.

Pancho answered, 'Señor, I know how you have often told me that you like to meet fellow Americanos so I have brought you one. He is a good man!'

The storekeeper swung round on his stool to face me. 'Well, stranger, any man that my friend here vouches for is good enough for me. Howdy!' and he stuck out a hand the size of a small ham for me to shake.

'Lomass is the name. Pete Lomass. I'm a writer for several American newspapers.'

'Lomass, eh? I've read a number of your articles and like your style. What brings you down into Mexico?'

As I prepared to answer his question, I noticed a well-worn crutch leaning against the wall behind him and realized that during the conversation he never stood up from his stool. I hazarded a guess.

'Well sir, I came down here looking for a man with an interesting story. And I think that today I've found him, Mr Bill Syke!'

He burst out laughing so heartily that I joined him, as did Pancho. 'So you think that you've found Bill Syke do you? Well, maybe you're right 'cos that was my name, although I have another registered with the Mexican authorities. What can I do for you, Pete?'

I pulled out my notepad and flipped it open to the page on which was written the poem about the Dogleg shootout. I told Bill how I had first encountered this torn from an ages-old newspaper and how, being piqued with curiosity, I had decided to seek more information and the interesting paths into which it led me. I handed the notepad to Bill and remained silent while he read through it and then appeared to read it through once more. Finally, with a strange half-smile, he handed the notepad back to me and sat there with a faraway look in his eyes.

He turned to me and apologized for his long silence. 'Sorry Pete! You have no idea of the plethora of memories this poem brings forth. I was just trying to marshal my thoughts, so that I could present them in a coherent manner. If you don't mind, perhaps we could sit at a table while I tell my story.'

He opened a flap in the counter to allow exit and, seizing his crutch, propelled himself forward to one of the tables where he seated himself heavily. The two *Rurales* in the corner had either finished their game, or were disgusted with the competing noise, got up and without a word departed. When they had gone Bill exclaimed, 'Good! Now I can talk without fear of interruption. Do you mind if I just tell the story my way? I may ramble on a bit but bear with me.'

'Bill! You just tell the story whichever is the best way for you. I'll just take notes if you don't mind,' and I settled down, pen in hand to receive Bill's account.

'Well I was born and spent my early years on a hard-scrabble farm in Indiana. When I was about ten, Pa got the wanderlust to travel west and make his fortune. So Ma and Pa and we three youngsters, of whom I was the oldest, travelled west, first by train and then by wagon. Pa never did find the pot of gold at the end of the rainbow. He worked on farms, in mines, clerked in stores and in town offices, but he just didn't seem to strike a job which allowed him to succeed.

'Eventually, with a little bit of savings he tried his hand at homesteading in western New Mexico. He and Ma built the cabin in which we lived and we survived by subsistence farming. We grew enough foodstuffs and raised enough animals to keep us fed, but there was never enough to sell and make a profit. By this time I was twelve going on thirteen and could do my share of the chores. In addition, I did some trapping, not much, but enough to bring in a dollar or two to help the family pot.

'One day when I was away from the cabin a small bunch of raiding Apaches – Mescaleros, I later learned – passed by. They were out for devilment and had already killed a Mexican sheepherder further down the valley. Well, without going into the ghastly details they killed Ma and Pa and my two younger brothers and I returned from my trapping to find my family massacred and the cabin in flames.

'As I was sitting, stunned at the loss of my family, I

81

heard a voice singing among the trees. I quickly hid and none too soon as a solitary Apache came in sight singing a victory chant. I later figured out that he was of the same party that had attacked the cabin and that he had returned to see if there was anything worth taking to his wickiup. Searching for loot, he put his weapon down as he lifted a charred board to see what it concealed.

'I approached, bent on vengeance, but he saw me and darted for his rifle. Fortunately, I reached the spot before him and grabbing the gun, I found the trigger just as he seized the weapon to tear it from my grip. His rifle was between us, vertical, in a near parody of a military present arms position. Luckily for me a round was already chambered and I cocked and fired in one movement. The gun bellowed and the round exited the chamber, scorching my shirt-front as it did so. Passing between us, it struck the Apache underneath the jaw and continuing upward passed through his brain and blew out the back of his head.

'Suddenly, I had a dead Indian in my arms and I lowered him to the ground with a great feeling of revulsion. I have read a number of accounts where people experienced all kinds of remorse after the death of a fellow human being, regardless of whether he was a sworn enemy or a total stranger. Well, I can honestly state that my emotion was purely one of relief at having killed one of a party that had destroyed my family.

'The rifle now in my possession was a Henry .44

calibre that fired rim-fire cartridges, already dated by the Winchester centre fire gun said to have "won the West". Still the Henry, though firing a lighter load, carried up to sixteen rounds in its tube magazine below the barrel and for a lad who hitherto only possessed a hunting knife was more than adequate.

'The Henry was in very good condition, leading me to believe that it had until recently been the property of some luckless settler but there was no marking to indicate its origin. Searching the body I found a bag with thirty-five more cartridges and another knife, which I appropriated and then with a half-burnt shovel I dug a hole in which to bury my poor family. That accomplished and the grave site marked with a crude cross and piled with stones to discourage animals from digging it up, I set out to track down the murderers.

'When you really think about it I was extremely foolish. A young half-grown boy on the trail of an unknown number of hardened killers who have already murdered and would have no qualms in doing so again. Furthermore, although I was a country-grown lad with a knowledge of tracking and bush-craft, I was a complete tyro compared to the training my foes would have received while being raised.

'I found them on the third day. It was early evening and they were seated around a small camp-fire in a hollow among the rocks, busy passing a flask back and forth between them. I settled down to watch as they sank deeper into a drunken stupor and with the last light of the day I shot all four of them,

pouring in rounds from that Henry as fast as I could
work the loading lever. It was not an heroic deed, Mr
Lomass! Rather it was the act of a grief-stricken boy
thinking that regardless of possible consequences, he
had to avenge the death of his family. Only one of
the Apaches moved as I executed them. He rose to
his feet befuddled with the mescal he had consumed
and fell riddled across the campfire. I reloaded as
fast as I could and seeing no movement, retreated
from that bowl of death and kept going until I was
many miles from the area.

'The next few years I wandered across the West,
finding work wherever it was available. Gradually I
developed the skills of a cowhand and became recognized as a dependable competent addition to any
ranch as I always rode for the brand. During those
years, two of the outfits for which I rode became
involved in range wars. It was impossible to remain
aloof and somehow, despite my own desires, I gained
the unenviable reputation of being fast with a gun of
any type.

'That prompted me to move east and then south
and one day I found myself pounding on the door of
a cabin which was the headquarters of Agnes
Burton's Bar 6 ranch, down west of the Mojave River.
Old mister Burton had cashed in his chips, leaving
Agnes as sole owner of the ranch and she was finding
the running of an outfit was no easy matter.

'I developed a great respect and liking for Agnes
Burton. I never even attempted to develop our relationship any further. Josh Mortimer the foreman, a

grand guy, had already set his cap in that direction so we all just remained very good pards. Eventually, as you know, Agnes and Josh got married and I became the foreman of the Bar 6. Together we built up the ranch so that we were running about six thousand beeves under the care of nine cowhands, including yours truly.

'We were a happy ranch, Mr Lomass. You know some outfits can be super-efficient yet there is still something missing. The hands do their tasks but there is not too much joy abounding. The Bar 6 was different. Each and every cowhand was interested in every improvement that was made, the boys joshed and kidded each other all day long and would gather outside the bunkhouse in the evening singing those old Stephen Foster songs that we knew so well. Those were indeed happy days.

'Then Mike Carstairs, or Dapper Mike as he became known, appeared on the scene. He became the permanent gambler at Red Corcoran's saloon and all that entered were slowly encouraged to play cards with him. Initially he was all smiles, offering a mild, friendly game involving little or no money. Then later the stakes rose and so did the challenging cries as he sought to get the boys to his card table. A common refrain was, 'Come on, boys, let's have a little flutter or is Mamma still controlling the little fella's purse strings!' This, said in a jeering voice was enough of a challenge to get them seated.

'I told the boys that Mike also cheated. I knew it but though I watched carefully while not actually playing with the man, I never was able to catch him in the act. The thing that actually got the fat in the fire though was an event that happened not in the saloon, but actually on the main street of Dogleg.

'Miss Agnes had gone into town in the Surrey to do some small shopping. She had taken young Pat O'Rourke with her as escort and he remained with the team while she did her womanly purchases. As she came out of the millinery store she was accosted by Dapper Mike, who had never encountered her before. He stepped in front of her forcing her to stop and, when she side-stepped to go around him, he did the same again, thwarting her progress. Then, raising his hat sarcastically, he introduced himself and made inappropriate comments regarding Agnes' mode of dress and her hidden figure. All this was unacceptable to a decent woman, but then he went completely beyond the pale, grabbing her by the arm and suggesting that they go up to his room to get better acquainted.

'Now Agnes Burton was a good, healthy, farm-bred girl with a goodly amount of muscle for one of the fair sex and at his foul words she reacted accordingly. Shrugging herself free of his grasp, she delivered an open-handed slap to his face that sent him staggering back against the store window.

'Before he could react, Pat had leapt from the Surrey and running forward stuck his pistol in Mike's gut with a cry of, "Just one little move, mister, and you're dead meat!" and he forced Mike to apologize to Miss Agnes in front of the gathering crowd.

'Mike was furious at having to back down in public, but that cocked .45 calibre Colt revolver sticking in his midriff was a great incentive and so he babbled a half-hearted excuse for his uncouth behaviour and was then allowed to go on his way.

'Of course, when Pat and Agnes returned home the story was quickly spread among the remaining hands, with the result that the ill-blood between the boys of the Bar 6 and Dapper Mike had reached fever point. I should point out that Agnes and Josh Mortimer had been married for some time by now but to the hands, she was still their girl in a sisterly way. They all cared for her and would willingly fight for her also. Anyway, Mr Lomass, I think you can see that the stage was set for the events that were described in the poem.

'It was pay day, the hands had all been paid and Josh had given them a twenty-dollar bonus, in view of the sale of cattle to MacTavish, that Scotsman ranching west of us. A group of us accompanied Josh to Dogleg when he went to deposit his money from the sale of the cattle in the bank and, as you know, from there we went to have a drink at Big Red's.

'So we come to the time of the big shootout when it seemed that the world went mad.' Bill suddenly ceased in his reminiscences as a door opened in the rear of the store and a slightly built woman emerged.

'Bill!' she paused, suddenly aware there were other people present. She continued, 'Bill, supper is ready. Should I prepare for guests or are we dining alone?'

Pancho immediately announced that he had to return to his camp. 'You stay, Pedro. I think that you will find it interesting. *Adíos*, my friend.' He shook my hand. '*Hasta la vista*!' and was gone.

Bill Syke sat there smiling as I turned and indicated that it would be a great pleasure to have dinner here. 'In that case, Pete, I think we had better have some formal introductions! My dear, this is Pete Lomass. He is a well-known reporter and war correspondent. Pete, I want you to meet my wife Jenny. Formally known as Jenny Ling.'

My jaw hung open as I gingerly took the slim little hand that was extended to me. 'I am indeed pleased to meet you, ma'am. Bill will tell you what a series of weird adventures I've had in connection with the name of Jenny Ling.'

I was escorted through the back of the store to a comfortably appointed living room where, in an alcove beyond, Jenny engaged in her culinary skills to eventually provide extra food for the unexpected guest.

While she was thus busy, Bill kept up an abbreviated account of my experiences to date spent trying to unearth the origins of the poem about the Dogleg shootout. Jenny indicated by monosyllabic responses that the preparation of the dishes was of premier importance. To which, based upon the delicious odours coming forth, I was duty-bound to agree.

Shortly after we sat down to a great dinner of chicken, fried the Southern way, with lashings of creamy mashed potatoes, beans in sauce and green vegetables mixed with baby carrots, accompanied by some of the best hot biscuits I have ever tasted. This repast, washed down with cups of black sweet coffee, certainly made up for the limited fare at Pancho Villa's camp!

CHAPTER ELEVEN

After dinner with the dishes cleared away, we sat and I listened to Jenny Ling tell her story.

'You should know, Mr Lomass, that I am half Chinese. My mother was sold by her parents in China to a Chinese trader who dealt in such merchandise. She, along with a number of girls in similar circumstances, was brought to the port of San Francisco under the guise of potential house servants, although I suspect that the port officials knew what was happening, but turned a blind eye in return for a cut in the profits.

'My mother was sold at a secret auction, attended only by wealthy white men, to a John Henreid and she became his sex slave for the next three years until he tired of her. In the second year of her bondage, I was born. And I suspect that this was one of the reasons that Mr Henreid decided to rid himself of my mother. He didn't want to be known as the father of a half-breed.

'My mother knew that we had to get away, other-wise she would end up in one of the many bordellos in the city and she would lose me. Secretly, over a long period of time, she had stolen from Henreid a few coins at a time so that he would not miss them and, when ready, she just walked out as though just taking her baby for a stroll. And she kept going.

'She could not trust any of our people. Most of them were so poor that the thought of protecting a runaway would not occur to them, but the notion of a reward would. And the richer ones would sell any-thing and anyone to increase their profits. So she just kept going, switching from train to wagons, moving us repeatedly so as to confuse any pursuit.

'She did this repeatedly while picking up odd jobs working in laundries, kitchens and in isolated ranch houses, anything to make a few coins to keep us going. Finally, in a small town in western Colorado she obtained a position as cook with a pastor and his wife and there we stayed for several years.

'Meanwhile, I was growing and Mrs Billings per-suaded Momma that I should go to school and in fact paid the fees. Thus, I learned to read and write, and in many ways became a little American girl. All was well until one day Momma collapsed in the kitchen. The doctor said she had a cancer and he was right. Apparently she had been in pain for many months past and had a very short time in which to live.

'Well she died, and Pastor Billings arranged for me to be sent to the church orphanage in Colorado Springs. I didn't want to go, but was sent anyway, and there I stayed until I was about fifteen, when I decided to go forth on my own.

'I had always enjoyed singing and at the orphanage used to sing at our concerts which, being open to certain members of the public, meant that my performance was applauded not only by the staff but also by outsiders. Therefore, I thought, in my childish innocence, that I could make my way in the world by singing.

'It didn't quite work out that way. I wasn't professionally trained, and didn't have a hope in Hades of obtaining such training and therefore could only find work in cheap music halls or singing in saloons. And in both types of locations the patrons and my fellow performers intimated that I could make more money lying on my back than in singing. I ignored them, but it was hard as I drifted from town to town and eventually ended up in Dogleg, Texas.

'I started working for Red Corcoran about six months after Dapper Mike appeared on the scene. Mr Red always treated me as a young lady and was very kind, but Mike! He was absolutely horrible, always making lewd remarks and not merely hinting but stating publicly that I was actually a young whore playing hard to get. I wasn't, Mr Lomass, and he was disgusting.'

Here, Jenny displayed a certain degree of

emotion, so Bill Syke broke in to remove some of the pressure she was experiencing. 'As a matter of fact, Pete, confidentially, Jenny was never like that at all and no man had had his way with her until she was wed. Jenny and I were in time married in that little church across the square and our union was duly recorded in the parish register. So, whoever wrote that poem either didn't know what he was talking about, or deliberately set about smearing Jenny's good name.'

Jenny continued, 'Mr Lomass, I've only one more thing to add. Shortly before the night of the fire, Mike tried his oily approach on me, suggesting that we could both have a good time on the wealth he expected to inherit. He never said where this money was going to be coming from, merely that he fully expected it to be so.'

Bill took up the narrative. 'I think that the mayhem that broke out in Red's Saloon was a deliberate provocation. Mike had indeed bought himself a gang that night, bestowing free drinks to some of his cronies. He had gathered a number of gun-toting characters about him quite willing to do as he wished.

'When he made the derogatory remark about Jenny, it was almost like a signal for his gang to respond to the Bar 6 reaction. I think that it was young Pat O'Rourke who ordered him to withdraw the remark. Pat was hot-headed and already spoiling for a fight over Mike's treatment of Miss Agnes, but Pat did not take the first shot. That came from the other side of the saloon and nicked me in the left shoulder.

'I drew my '75 Remington and fired a wild shot in the direction from whence the bullet that clipped my shoulder had come. Pat may have done the same as his pistol was still emitting a tendril of smoke as I turned back in time to see the barman level his sawn-off at O'Rourke's back. I was just seconds too late. The blast, as he let young Pat have both barrels, sent the lifeless body of that young cowboy several feet as he was thrown to the floor. The barman was still grinning as I put a bullet right between his eyes.

'By that time, and, Pete, you've got to understand everything was happening in seconds that night, Josh had gone to speak to Red about closing the bar and both of them had been shot at the same time. That double killing was no accident. Their murder was a premeditated act by Mike and one of his henchmen.

'Meanwhile, as the poem says, the shooting had become general. The room was filled with thick, grey smoke (you must remember that back then nobody had smokeless powder) and people were just firing through the gloom at muzzle flashes. The fire from the downed chandelier had started to spread across the floor and there was a simultaneous stampede for the door.

'I yelled for Ernie to give a hand and, together with Cherokee and José, we picked up the body of Josh Mortimer, our boss, and, together, we got out of that blazing inferno. As we did so there was fresh gunfire aimed at us from the Mercantile, and the four of us left Josh's body and attempted to deal with that fresh situation.

'And so it continued through the night as the town burned around us. I had lost sight of Dapper Mike early on as the fracas developed and then later I spotted him near the bank as that building too went up in flames. By that time I had become separated from the other Bar 6 boys and was becoming increasingly concerned as to their safety.

'We were all wounded in one way or another. In my own case I had received at least four bullet wounds; the one in the shoulder, a furrow across the ribs and another from wrist to left elbow and a bullet lodged in my right leg above the knee.

'Anyway, I had ended up, as the poem says, in a corral at the end of town where Old Ezra Perkins kept his mules. A sliver of silvery light along the eastern horizon indicated that the dawn of yet another day was momentarily upon us as I rested leaning upon the horizontal poles of the corral, punching out the empty cases from my pistol and reloaded my Remington.

'Then I saw Mike and at the same time I believe he saw me. He was staggering along, weighed down by two heavy saddle bags which he dropped as soon as he saw me and went for his pistol, secured in a Huckleberry holster. We both must have fired at about the same time. I thought at the time that I had delivered a killing shot that knocked him off his feet, but my bullet must have been deflected by something, a watch or maybe a deck of cards in his breast pocket.

'His shot had smashed into my right hip tearing up the joint so badly that, although I recovered, that hip was forever useless. That's when Jenny came along. Whoever wrote that poem did not know what actually happened, or was still determined to smear her good name. Jenny approached some Chinese laundry workers cowering in a ditch and, using her linguistic skills, persuaded them to carry me to a hut some distance from the town where she attended to my wounds until they were seen by a doctor. Then she bought a tent in which I lived while she nursed me back to health.

'Outside of my limited sickbed world, people began trying to rebuild their lives. Agnes and the boys from the Bar 6 came to see me and she in particular urged me to return to the ranch, but it was not practical. At that moment I was too sick to move and, even if I made a complete recovery, of what use would I – a cripple – be on a ranch? So I declined all the kind offers and entreaties and remained in our tent until we left Dogleg.

'Nobody had seen anything of Dapper Mike since the shootout. Somebody spread the rumour that he had perished in the fire but that wouldn't wash, since the poem put him firmly in Ezra's corral the following morning. Ezra himself may have known what actually happened but he remained silent and indeed may have received cash for doing so. From all the reports that I heard, Ezra had acquired some money at the time of the fire, but became reclusive and scared of his own shadow thereafter.

'It's possible that the story of him getting religion at the Big Tent Revival meeting may have prompted him to search his conscience if indeed he had witnessed a crime but had failed to report it, and if so may have led to his unpleasant death. I guess we will never know.

'Equally the fate of Dapper Mike has remained a secret all of these years. I have suspected that he has tried to locate me and Jenny here from time to time either for some imagined need for revenge or to silence us because he thinks that we know something of his criminal past, and that is why I spread the word around El Paso years ago that we did not want to be found.

'That brings me to one final point, Pete. I'm not scared of anything Mike could do to me but I do have Jenny to think of. How much of this story are you going to write?'

'Bill, to tell you the truth I'm not on assignment. I have six months leave of absence from the paper and started this search purely out of idle curiosity. Since then I've been shot at and it has become a personal vendetta. I don't know how it will end but will certainly do nothing to endanger the well-being of people that I've come to like and admire.'

Bill Syke indicated, as did Jenny sitting quietly by, that my words were enough assurance for them and with that we brought the evening to a close. Since it was late, too late to go forth seeking a night's lodging, the Sykes made up a bed for me in a little store room off the living room and there I spent the night, restlessly dreaming of gunfights as distorted images based upon our conversations flickered through my over-active brain.

CHAPTER TWELVE

In the morning Jenny served both me and Bill with a breakfast fit for a king and, when Martinez turned up, I prepared to bid farewell to these two Americans who had opened their door and their hearts to me. A firm handshake from Bill, a tight hug from Jenny who stood silently with tears gathering in her eyes, a quick 'So long, folks' and I was gone out of their lives.

Martinez had a horse waiting for me and I mounted, assuming that we would return to the bandit hide-out. Instead that wily Mexican led me through the village to a location where the rail lines passed through a deep cutting in the hillside. There was a plate-layer's hut right beside the track and, having dismounted, there we waited inside away from prying eyes.

I really had no idea what was going on except for the fact that plans were made to deliver me either back to Juarez or to Chihuahua City. Martinez was the strong silent type who either shrugged his shoulders when asked a question, or responded with a curt, '*No sé!*' ('I don't know!')

The hut was solidly built of discarded railroad ties and had a rough seat nailed to one wall. There was a small stove upon which the workers could boil water or cook a simple meal and upon which currently a pot of dubious-looking coffee was simmering away.

We had been in the hut for less than an hour when there was a sound of noise outside and a rough voice issued a command in Spanish. When the order was repeated more slowly in an even louder tone I looked at Martinez and enquired, '*Rurales?*'

He looked at me and smiled, shaking his head slowly. 'No, Señor! Juan Gomez, and other enemies of Pancho Villa!'

I had been so preoccupied with the thoughts regarding the conversation of the previous evening that I hadn't paid attention to Martinez' attire. He was wearing a poncho similar to that of Villa and at a quick glance could be mistaken for the bandit leader as long as his face was in shadow. Come to think of it, the horse Martinez normally rode was a dapple grey, whereas his steed of this morning seemed an off-white, created I now realized by a generous application of whitewash! But why? That question was answered almost immediately. The voice outside spoke once more.

'Hey, Villa! I've got you surrounded! Come out with your hands up and we will talk! I give you until I have counted to ten and then we will start shooting.

I know that you are in there with the gringo, you hear me!'

Martinez' response to this was to break the glass of the window and trigger two shots in the general direction of Mexico City. I meanwhile had dug into my grip and produced my Colt, thinking that if we two were going to make a last stand I might as well join in.

While preparing to add my firepower to that of Martinez, I was thinking furiously about the situation and came to the realization that we had been deliberately set up to fall into this trap.

There was a fusillade of shots from the men outside, only one of which entered the hut through the window. The others could be heard thudding into the thick walls of the hut and I gave silent thanks to the men who had constructed the building out of railroad ties. Still if the men outside wasted enough ammunition they could chew through the walls, which was not a happy thought!

Martinez and I took it in turns to carefully stand obliquely to the window and fire the odd shot towards the side of the cutting where Gomez and his men were hidden. I didn't stay exposed long enough to see anything and I doubt whether, except by random chance, we actually hit anyone.

Time passed, and then there was a definite change in the situation. There was a far-off thunder of hoof beats rapidly drawing nearer, followed by confused shooting and an uproar of voices. Martinez' face no longer had its dour scowl but was now wreathed in a wide grin as he declared, 'Villa comes!'

The shooting finally stopped and moments later a well-known voice called out, '*Hola*, my friend Pedro! You can come out now. It is quite safe!'

Cautiously, I opened the door to the hut and peered out. That damned bandit was sitting there on his white horse, as happy as a sand boy with the success of his stratagem to rid himself of his rivals in that part of Chihuahua.

I was furious to think that Martinez and I had been staked out for the sole purpose of eliminating the bandits who vied with Villa for control in these mountains. Actually, by this time I was convinced that Martinez knew exactly what was going on and it was only the dumb gringo, namely Pete Lomass, who was kept entirely in the dark.

'Pancho, you lousy bastard! You used me to set a trap for some more of your miserable fraternity!' I cussed him in English, in Spanish and in half a dozen other languages, describing him, his genealogy, and all his associates!

And all the while he sat there on that big white horse and laughed at me. 'Pedro! Don't take it to heart. You were never in any danger. There were my people watching over you ever since you left the good Bill Syke. You are my good friend, Pedro. Come, let us bid farewell as true friends with no bitterness between us.' He pointed to three bodies lying on the ground. 'I just did what had to be done!' Mollified somewhat, I took the hand that he offered down to me and shook it heartily. 'Now we must get you on a train, my gringo friend.'

The far-off whistle of an approaching locomotive produced a hive of activity as the corpses were removed from the scene, as were many of the horses and men until eventually there was just Villa, Martinez, myself and three other bandits waiting by the plate-layer's hut.

The train drew nearer and as it rounded a bend I saw to my dismay that it was a long line of trucks laden, no doubt, with all sorts of merchandise and with a red caboose bringing up the end. There were no passenger cars.

'Pancho! This is no good! I need a train with passenger cars!'

'Don't worry, Pedro! Everything will be as you Yankees say, h'OK.'

The train slowed and finally halted with a great cloud of expended steam. We rode along to the caboose and Pancho declared, 'Señor Pedro. Here is your private car. All is arranged. The brakeman is one of us. When you get to Juarez two men there will escort you to the bridge which leads to El Paso. After that you will be on your own. *Hasta la vista*, my very good friend!'

Pancho Villa raised his sombrero in a circular flourish as he turned away and in a few moments he had gone from my life, and I continued to try and unravel the mystery of the Dogleg shootout while he went on to become an immortalized figure of the Mexican revolution.

103

CHAPTER THIRTEEN

The caboose was comfortable and the brakeman and his assistant could not do enough for me, continually pressing me to have drinks of tequila and partake of delicacies prepared by their womenfolk. All in all, the journey north seemed to take no time at all and, suddenly, we were steaming into the goods yard of the Juarez Junction.

As arranged, two men met me and escorted me across the city to the bridge leading into El Paso and, an hour later, I was propping up the bar of the Sunrise Hotel, quaffing an American beer poured for me by Harry the barman. Mindful of my agreement with Bill Syke, I was reticent regarding the trip into Mexico except to say that it was moderately successful. I knew that Harry was sound but the less he knew, the less could be extracted from him!

I was forcibly reminded of the need for secrecy long before the evening was out. The saloon was still relatively empty when two men came in and strode up to the bar. They were dressed as workmen. Their clothing was rough and stained with oil and tar and each man wore heavy work boots.

Now, I'm not a snob. I'll drink with any man and have done so all over the world in many peculiar places. But an inner sense told me there was something fishy about this pair and the way in which they sidled along the bar, each movement bringing them closer to me. Therefore with their next sideways move I too moved four or five feet to my right and waited to see if they would try and repeat their manoeuvre. If so I would know that their actions were deliberate. They did so and I knew then that they would try and pick a fight with me.

I was a pretty good scrapper in those days and I decided that the old Roman dictum 'Let he who would have peace, prepare for war!' was appropriate under the present circumstances. As one of the toughs raised his glass to his lips I took a pace to my left and, nudging with my left elbow, struck his right arm spilling the liquid down his shirt front. I followed the nudge up with an aggressive remark of, 'What the hell did you do that for, you clumsy idiot!' and pointed down towards his boot. His eyes automatically followed my pointing finger and I delivered an upper cut that knocked him back and over a table. His companion had had time to haul out a blackjack and raised it with the intent of knocking out one of my eyes or in some way disabling me. Instead of cowering as expected, I stepped forward, placing my right arm behind his upper member and, blocking his forearm with my own, I grasped my right hand with the left one and applied considerable pressure to the arm holding the cosh.

The inevitable happened. His weight forward meeting my weight back caused him to drop the weapon and he screamed as his right elbow dislocated under the combined pressure. He stood there mewing like a cat holding the injured limb, staring at me in horror and at his companion deep in slumber on the floor.

Harry produced a jug of water and brought stiff number one back to consciousness by applying a liberal quantity of the liquid on his dirty face. He staggered to his feet. I delivered a parting shot and was not too surprised to see a glint of recognition as I ordered, 'Now get out of here and go back to Mike and tell him I don't scare easily. Now go!'

They slunk out of the saloon and Harry turned to me with relief written all over his face. 'Phew! I'm glad that's over. Mr Lomass, where on earth did you learn to fight that dirty?'

'Well, Harry, in my travels all over the world as a correspondent I've ended up in some mighty strange places and was forced to learn how to defend myself by fair means and foul if need be. This was one of those occasions. Those men came in here to deliberately beat me up, I know the type, and I didn't desire a beating, hence my initiative.'

We both agreed that I would have to be on my guard at all times and on that note I went up to my room and prepared for bed, not forgetting to jam a heavy chair under the doorknob to discourage any uninvited callers from gaining entry. Despite the recent turmoil I had a sound, dreamless night and arose the next morning refreshed and eager for that first cup of coffee.

Hardly had I finished a good early breakfast when a man arrived in the lobby with the news that he had my Ford down in the street all repaired and serviced, gassed up and ready for me. He presented a bill for fifty-one dollars, which I thought was very reasonable, and having paid that and settled up with the hotel manager I left, not forgetting to strap on my holster containing my .45 Colt.

CHAPTER
FOURTEEN

As I negotiated the El Paso streets leading eastward and while part of my mind struggled with the mechanical exertion coupled with the need to avoid errant pedestrians and the odd livestock roaming the highways, I was also struck by the irony of the fact that I travelled into Mexico visibly unarmed, yet returning to my own country I felt the need to have a firearm handy.

The day was overcast and as I left the city behind I halted and rapidly swung the canvas tonneau into place. I was none too soon as shortly thereafter we were engulfed in a typical southern deluge, which flooded the ruts and potholes of the dirt track masquerading as a highway. Some time earlier I had had one of those manually operated windshield wipers installed and today it really paid for itself. So, as we lurched skidded and splashed from one pothole to the next I performed an act like a one-armed wallpaper hanger, steering one handed while simultaneously manipulating the little handle that controlled the wiper.

Gradually the storm tapered off and the visibility improved, though such was the condition of the track that I didn't dare to proceed at any speed other than at a crawl. The sun appeared which was a most welcome sight and so as we crept along I ate my lunch while driving. Harry the barman had arranged last night for me to be given a packed lunch of sandwiches when I left the hotel and these, together with a flask of cold coffee, furnished me with a late morning meal.

The highway was deserted, other travellers having a great deal more common sense than yours truly to go out gallivanting on such a miserable day. Therefore, I had the track to myself and, being alone, I often chose the surface which appeared to furnish the better driving condition and thus drove in a seemingly erratic manner, swinging to the left and then to the right while at the same time being very conscious of the overflowing ditches on either side.

Hours later, with my arms aching from the effort of wrestling with the steering wheel, I drove slowly down the main street of Dogleg Crossing and halted outside the Eatery.

I went in and found the place almost deserted, except for a couple of kitchen staff cleaning up after late midday diners. Initially, there was no sign of Jane and then she came from the kitchen with her head turned away as she completed the giving of some instruction to one of the cooks. Then she turned her head and noticed me standing quietly by the door.

'Pete!' she breathed as she hurried over to me and, ignoring the staff, literally threw herself into my open arms. 'Oh Pete! Where have you been? I know that it's only a few days since you left Dogleg but it seems ages since I last saw you. And there was no word of what you were doing. I began to imagine all sorts of things had happened to you and eventually wondered if you had left Dogleg for good and had forgotten me!'

I raised my right hand and gently put my fingers across her lips stifling her queries. 'Not now, Jane! I have lots to tell you, but it will wait 'til later. Now, how have you been and what seems to have got you so worked up and, thirdly could you spare a cup of coffee for a weary traveller?'

Jane nodded and left my arms, unwillingly I thought, and moments later I was seated at a table with a thick wedge of apple pie and a steaming hot mug of coffee before me. She seated herself across the table from me and waited patiently while I demolished the pie and drank the coffee and also downed a second mug.

'Well, Jane, I have a lot of information to tell you but this is neither the time nor the place. At this moment you'll just have to be content with the news that I went to El Paso to get the windshield of my automobile repaired and, while there, decided to take a little side trip into Mexico while the work was being done on the car. And that's basically it. The car was delivered to me very early this morning and I headed back to see you immediately.'

I could see that my bland explanation of my absence was not going to wash with Jane but it would have to suffice until we were alone. With staff members walking back and forth in the Eatery there was no telling what shreds of our conversation could be picked up and therefore I intended, which was not very difficult, to keep the appearance of my meeting with Jane purely on a romantic level.

I smiled at her and gently squeezed her hand under the table, to which I was happy to note she responded. 'Must get along, Jane. I need to clean up after the long drive and have other things which are demanding my attention.' Then whispering, 'See you tonight! Your place!' I stood up and blowing her a kiss, stepped outside.

My room behind the Lucky Dollar saloon was untouched, as were the few things that I'd left there and so I had a quick wash and shave before parking the Ford in an open shed and setting forth to see the town once more.

On a whim I dropped into the cantina and ordering a tequila, had a brief chat with Pablo behind the bar. With him, the situation was little changed. Juanita his daughter was still enamoured with Jim Rossiter, who was still overbearing and brash in his dealing with the girl and her father. I listened patiently while Pablo enumerated the many problems

111

borne by a Mexican father attempting to raise a beautiful but wilful daughter and, after agreeing that if I ever married I would adopt a different course of action in raising a child, managed to turn the conversation to other topics.

'Pablo! Have there been any changes in Dogleg while I have been away? For example, has anyone been asking for me?' I reminded him of the situation that was beginning to show itself before I left, where some people were going around suggesting that as a newspaperman I was stirring up trouble.

He paused in his task of stacking glasses on the counter-top and obviously considered my question seriously. 'No, Señor Lomass! I have not heard anyone saying bad things about you. I think that started because you made a certain Texan back down over a bottle of beer and he was trying to. . . .' he paused, 'what you say, get his own back on you. Oh, I forget! There were two men in town asking about you. I don't know who they were, but I think that maybe they were police or something.'

I thanked Pablo for the information and left, strolling down the street to the telegraph office. As I walked I pondered over Pablo's information. *Hmm! Two men looking for me. Could be police or other officials? Who could they be?*

There were two messages waiting for me. One was from my editor lauding me on the article about Pancho Villa and asking for more. In typical telegraph jargonese he stated, 'Great story re Bandit. Tell more. Good way to spend vacation!' Well, any

further visits into Mexico would have to wait, Boss!
I'm now on a different trail.

The other, a voice from the dead, was from poor
Joe Dolan, sent before he met his untimely end. The
message was merely to the effect that Michael
Carstairs, alias Dapper Mike, had spent time in a New
York jail for theft and also that he was still wanted for
questioning in the case of a young girl, a dancer
found dead in mysterious circumstances. The case
had remained open on the books although the crime
had occurred twenty-two years ago.

So, it would appear that Dapper Mike had started
his life of crime long before he headed west and now
we had a probable murder added to his list.

CHAPTER FIFTEEN

On an impulse I went into the bank and asked to see the manager. After a short wait I was shown into his office and introduced myself as I gave him my card. He studied it as he asked me to sit and I in my turn studied him.

He looked to be about the same age as myself, that is in the late thirties or early forties. A trifle portly with a protruding stomach, no doubt created by a life of sitting behind a desk, he was about my height of close on six feet. His florid features were indicative of a man who liked his food and, with a clean-shaven face and a closely clipped grey moustache to match his grey hair, Mr Barnard exuded the air of a successful businessman.

'What can I do for you, Mr Lomass? I am, of course, familiar with a number of your exciting reports published in a number of the newspapers, but why did you wish to see me?'

'Mr Barnard, I'm not quite sure why I'm here but, if you can spare a few minutes of your time, perhaps you'd permit me to explain?'

'Well, Mr Lomass, I don't have an appointment until late this afternoon so I'm currently just tidying up some of the accounts. Yes, you just fire ahead and I'll stop you if I find I'm running short of time.'

I nodded and launched into an abbreviated account of the Dogleg shootout. I told him of the poem and produced my hand-written copy. He had heard of it, but had never seen a copy. I said that I had interviewed a number of the participants or survivors and wondered if there was anyone from the bank who had been around at that time.

To that query, Barnard shook his head. 'No, Mr Lomass. I've been here fifteen years and all the present staff came after me.' Then he brightened and said, 'Apart from old Jedediah that is! As I understand it old Jed was taken on as handyman and general factotum at the time that the bank was built. The first bank, that is. He's really past it now. Jed just comes in and potters around a bit and we give him a very small pension. Most of the time he calls me Mr Devries. That was the name of the manager who was here at the time of the fire. He's been dead may years!'

I dropped my bombshell. 'Mr Barnard, information has reached me that the Dogleg ruckus was all part of a deliberate plot to rob the bank. The robbers no doubt thought that in the confusion, the fire in the bank building would be considered just part of the general conflagration. Was there anything saved from the fire?'

115

Barnard delved into his filing cabinet and after searching, produced a rather dog-eared Manila folder which contained a number of documents. He adjusted his spectacles and commenced to read them one by one: 'Hmm. Bank losses. This one indicates that the bank was believed to have had $165,000 on deposit at the time of the fire. Of this sum, the vast majority was in United States paper currency with a small amount in British pounds sterling. There was also believed to have been $20,000 in gold coins, mainly $20 gold double eagles.

'When the fire had died down and it was safe enough for workers to enter the premises they found the door to the vault was open. Experts assumed that the intense heat of the fire had caused the door to burst open and the flames had consumed the paper money. The gold was in canvas sacks and these too had perished in the fire. There was evidently a general belief that the gold had actually melted during the fire and this would appear to have been the case since traces of gold were found when new foundations for this present building were being dug.

'The remainder of the papers are merely insurance claims, descriptions of furniture and equipment lost in the fire and quotes by the insurance adjuster when settling the claims. I hope that the data I've read out has been of some use to you, Mr Lomass,' and he rose to bring our meeting to a close.

As he did so, a clerk hurried in apologizing for

interrupting and exclaimed, 'I say, sir! A boy just came in with terrible news! Old Jed has just been found in an alley with his head bashed in! Who could do such a terrible thing?'

'Where did this happen?'

'Down the street by the side of the old Emporium building.'

'Well, you get back to your teller's wicket, Schwartz. I'm just going down the street with this gentleman and, as Senior Teller, you are now in charge. Come, Lomass, I think this may have a bearing on our discussion,' and seizing his hat and cane he led the way from the bank to an alley where already a small crowd had gathered. We pushed our way through to the front and were halted by a couple of Al Watson's deputies who were attempting to keep people back so that the doctor and the marshal himself could examine the body.

I meanwhile attempted to observe and note the general scene of the crime. Jed's body, clad in a pair of tattered jeans and a worn, striped shirt, lay on its stomach with the head twisted at an unnatural angle. His arms with the fingers tightly clenched were stretched out in front of him and a small pool of blood lay on the ground from the gaping wound at the back of the skull. The location was a typical alley strewn with discarded paper, empty cans, and with broken packing cases stacked along one wall. Any possible footprints had long since been destroyed underfoot by the actions of the people drawn as is so often the case to the scene of a murder, or indeed any tragedy.

The doctor stood up, wiping his hands on a cloth taken from his medical bag. 'Well, Marshal, it is obvious that you have a murder on your hands. From the state of Jed's body I would estimate that death took place some time last night. The curious thing is that the blow to the skull was unnecessary since his neck was already broken. It's almost as though the murderer wanted to make sure he was dead!'

A thought struck me and I started forward, introducing myself as I did so. 'Pete Lomass, reporter. Doctor, why are his hands so tightly clenched? Usually after death the hands relax. Is that not so?'

The doctor kind of half agreed and I continued, 'Does he have something in those hands, do you think?'

He shrugged his shoulders and stooping, opened the fingers of the left hand. Nothing but sandy soil from the ground of the alley. He repeated the procedure with the right hand and gasped. There in the palm lay a bright twenty-dollar double gold eagle.

'There, gentlemen, you have the motive for Jed's murder!' Turning to the bank manager, I continued in a lower voice, 'And there, quite possibly, proof that the bank was robbed twenty years ago during the fire.'

I left them discussing the crime and possible courses of action, retreating to my room behind the saloon. I needed time to think and the middle of a crowd was not the ideal location to engage in such an exercise.

To me it was obvious that Jed's murder was in some way linked to all the things that had happened to me ever since I started enquiring about the shootout at Dogleg Crossing. Oh, I'm not talking about my episode with Pancho Villa, although even that indirectly had a bearing since I was seeking survivors of the shooting. No, I'm thinking about the shots fired at me when I visited Jane Bronson's cottage. The attempt to ambush me while returning from the Bar 6 ranch. The intended attack upon me in El Paso and Jed's murder. Joe Dolan's murder. All were somehow linked and I suspected that Dapper Mike was the evil force behind these incidents. I was determined to be doubly on my guard.

CHAPTER SIXTEEN

Early evening, I figured that I should get some supper under my belt so strolled down to the Eatery. The place was medium full but I found a small table and sat down. A young waitress brought me coffee and later a meal. My mind was totally absorbed by the events of the day and, to tell the truth, I'm not even sure what I ordered. Probably chicken and dumplings followed by more of that delicious apple pie. If not that pie, then it's successor. Jane came over to confirm our meeting and after paying my bill, I left, strolling up Main Street and dropping into the saloon for a beer and a chat with the barman and anyone else propping up the bar.

When the hands of my pocket watch indicated nine forty-five, I downed the remainder of the drink that I had been nursing and walked down the street until, stopping in a doorway, I waited, observing the odd pedestrian until, at a moment when the street was clear, I slipped into an alley. Making my way by a combination of light from the cloud-obscured moon and feeling with either hand or foot, I slowly approached Jane's cottage.

I saw nobody and heard nothing as I sidled along the wall to the doorway and tapped lightly. Moments later a familiar voice whispered, 'Who's there?'

'It's me, Jane, Pete Lomass!' I whispered back and I heard two door bolts being withdrawn gently. The door opened but all inside was in darkness. I slipped in, the door closed and was locked and seconds later Jane was in my arms, smothering me with kisses and sobbing quietly with happiness and relief.

She led me to a couch in the darkness and for several more minutes we held each other until, finally, we separated and Jane lit a single lamp while composing herself to listen to all my news.

We settled down and I, with my right arm over her shoulder, gave her a detailed account of all my activities since I had driven off to visit the Bar 6. She gasped when I described in detail the attempted ambush and its conclusion and then described my subsequent adventures.

I did manage to obtain a laugh from her when I outlined my experiences with that ancient Oliver typewriter, but she grew silent and serious as I told her of the subsequent interview with Bill Syke and Jenny Ling, and was intrigued by the notion that they were happily married, tucked away in some isolated Mexican village.

When I mentioned my conclusions leading up to the recent murder of old Jed, Jane grasped my arm so tightly that I had to ease her fingers away as she was gouging with her sharp little nails.

'Now, Jane, I want to go back to the night of the fire. I know this is painful but it must be done. You and Beth were cleaning up the Bon Ton Café after a long day's work. Tell me more about Beth. Was she outgoing? Happy? Laughing and joking with the customers? Or was she the quiet pensive type of girl? Did she have any friends, male or female? I don't want to pry into the past, but somehow I think it is all interwoven. Tell me, Jane.'

She was silent for so long that eventually I wondered if she had gone to sleep but finally she gave a great big sigh and settling herself more comfortably, she began to answer my many queries.

'Well, Pete, actually, I was the serious one of us two girls. Beth in all truth was the most attractive and was tremendously popular, especially with all of the male customers. I guess that actually she was a bit of a flirt, but it was all in fun and neither she nor the male customer who was receiving her attention took it seriously. Oh, I'm sure that two or three had high hopes that, having set their caps in her direction, she would succumb to their blandishments, but it was not to be.

'Oh, there was one assignation about which Beth was very secretive. You must know, Pete, that girls are very sensitive about every aspect of their lives at that age and resent very strongly the notion that anyone is prying into their affairs. I guess in retrospect I was no different from poor Beth.

'This particular evening Beth seemed to take extra

care in the selection of her dress and in the application of her make-up. She left and returned in less than an hour. Her lipstick was badly smudged. She had somehow lost one glove and her dress was torn at the shoulder. In addition, I noticed from her reddened eyes that she had been crying.

'I didn't say a word. Beth would tell me in her own sweet time if she chose to do so and she never did. Life went on and she soon resumed her normal chatty, sweet-natured self.

'There is one curious thing, Pete. On the night of the fire Beth had stood up as a darkened silhouette appeared in the doorway. She may have spoken one word before he shot her. That word was "You!" The next moment he fired and she fell dead at my feet.'

Jane described for me how she had dragged Beth's body from the burning café and how in the morning neighbours had helped her to arrange a modest funeral. The shooting had been attributed to the general mayhem that occurred that awful night and Jane had been so busy attempting to rebuild her own life that gradually the death of Beth had receded into the far background.

We talked some more in generalities and finally I arose and indicated that it was time that I left. Jane also got up and we kissed each other passionately goodnight. The act being so pleasant we repeated it again and again until finally I, exerting my will against my own desires, pulled myself away and declared that I was leaving.

'Be careful!' whispered Jane as I slipped out of the

partially open door. I nodded, pulled my hat down over my eyes and sped silently across the wasteland that separated Jane's cottage and the backs of the buildings of Main Street. Hearing a slight noise, I half turned and as I did so I received a violent blow on the side of the head. It was a good thing that I half turned. As it was the blow glanced off my skull and I took part of the force on my left shoulder. If the full power behind that blow had been on an unprotected head I'm sure that I would have been killed the same way as poor Jed.

As it was there was a blinding flash and I was out for the count. I don't know how long I was lying there but recovered consciousness as an elderly lady was bathing my face and expressing sentiments of concern over my condition. She had apparently sent for additional help since the marshal and one of his deputies appeared as I rose groggily to my feet.

I must have been a real sight as he shone the light of a storm lantern upon my white countenance with blood streaming down the left side of my face. I had a thundering headache and just wanted to lay down again and sleep, which was a bad sign of a possible concussion.

'Lomass!' ejaculated Marshal Watson. 'What the hell happened to you?' He grasped me by the right arm and started to steer me towards the doctor's office, but I pulled away.

'See if Jane Bronson is OK before we worry about me!'

CHAPTER SEVENTEEN

Thanking the old lady who had rendered aid, I staggered over to Jane's cottage accompanied by Al Watson and his deputy. The door was ajar and calling out 'Jane!' we entered. The interior was in disarray. Al shone his lantern around. There was no sign of Jane but there was evidence that she had put up a fight before being subdued.

'Jane's been abducted!'

The words revolved around and around in my poor aching head. 'Al! We've got to get after them!'

'Hold on fella! You're in no condition to do anything at this moment. The very first thing that we've got to do is get you over to Doc Lawton's place and get you attended to.' And, after giving the deputy instructions on closing Jane's cottage up and leaving a man on guard he gently steered me to Doc Lawton's combined office and four-bed hospital.

The doc put three stitches in the side of my scalp

to close up the split there and also, as he wryly put it, to prevent my remaining brains from falling out! Then, after cleaning my face up and removing sundry pieces of gravel from the yard, he had me sit on a chair and shone lights in my eyes and observed me while I followed the movements of the pencil that he waved before me. At length he came to a conclusion.

'Well, Mr Lomass, there appears no medical evidence that you've suffered a concussion. Really, I should keep you here under observation for twenty-four hours but I imagine you'll object to that so all I can do is warn you to be careful.'

Thanking Dr Lawton and paying his modest bill, I walked with unsteady steps alongside Al Watson to the marshal's office where I sank exhausted in an office chair. Al busied himself washing a mug clean and then filling it with hot coffee, poured from the pot simmering away on the office stove. He then produced a bottle from a drawer in his desk and poured a liberal measure of whiskey into the coffee-filled mug. This libation was then offered to me with a marshal's diagnosis. 'Here, Lomass, get this inside you. I don't know much about medicine but I do know that a hot toddy will work wonders with whatever ails you. In fact I'll join you!' and he fixed a similar beverage for himself.

For a short while we sat in companionable silence while we sipped at the laced coffee and finally Al queried, 'So, Pete, if you don't mind me calling you by your first name, what do you make of all this? I know that you've been making enquiries around town. Is that what led to the attack on you? And also is Jane Bronson in danger?'

I had been thinking while Al prepared the coffee and had decided that I should lay out the full scenario so as to put him completely in the picture. Before I had a chance to commence, the door opened and in burst Jim Rossiter, my rival for the bottle of American beer!

'Lomass, are you OK? I was passing Pablo's when I heard what had happened to you. I sure hope that you don't think that I'm the kind of dirty rat who'd play at that kind of a game!' He turned to the marshal. 'If you're getting up a posse to go after the scum who've taken Miss Bronson, count me in!'

He seized my hand and shook it heartily. 'Lomass, you're OK. I know we had our little difference but that's all over. If you need me just holler!' and with that parting remark he was gone.

Al Watson and I looked at each other and smiled. Every ill wind brings some good with it and the present situation was no exception to the general rule. Having Jim Rossiter on our side was definitely an asset. He knew a lot of people and might possibly hear something that could aid us in the search for Jane that was getting underway.

Meanwhile, once more I told the whole story of the poem and my search for the individuals involved. I listed the various attacks upon myself here in Dogleg, on the way back from the Bar 6 ranch, and even in El Paso. 'Al, there is someone or some group of persons who just don't want any light thrown upon this subject.

'Take the murder of poor old Jed! Who would want to kill him? It's my guess that he somehow found out what happened to the gold which vanished from the bank at the time of the Dogleg shootout and was either killed because he wouldn't reveal what he knew or was just murdered so they could eliminate him!

'Al, I'm going to have to lay down for a short while. My head is pounding like a trip hammer, but I'll be OK shortly. You could do one thing for me which may help.' He looked at me questioningly. 'Swear me in as a special deputy. It may give me a little bit of authority when I'm roaming around asking questions.' He looked at me dubiously, but after some verbal persuasion did as I requested and thus I became a lawful badge-carrying deputy of Dogleg Crossing.

CHAPTER EIGHTEEN

I returned to my room behind the saloon and tried to rest a while. My head was continuing to pound although it was more like the monotonous boom of a deep bass drum; boom, boom, boom. My gut also felt decidedly queasy and I wondered if I was experiencing signs of concussion. Well, there was nothing that I could do about it so I just lay there in purgatory with my eyes closed.

As I lay there I thought continually of Jane and the mess that I'd landed her in. If I hadn't started this enquiry into the details of the Dogleg shootout she would have been still living her quiet life of running the Eatery and none of the mayhem would have involved her. Though not a religious man, I must confess that I prayed that someone up there was looking after her.

I lay quietly, half-covered by a sheet and tried to ignore that damned drum. But then a different sound crept into my senses. There was the sound of the door handle being slowly turned. When I had first taken the room I had complained about the lock being stiff and making a peculiar squeak. I was promised that it would be fixed but thankfully it never was. With the handle turned, the door began to open silently. I meanwhile had drawn my Colt and it lay grasped in my right hand alongside my body. A dark figure stood in the doorway and I watched him carefully through half-closed eyelids.

He stood there silently, watching me as though uncertain of his next move and, finally making up his mind, advanced upon my bed brandishing a large double-edged knife whose blade reflected the morning light from the window. As he reached the foot of the bed I sat up, levelling the Colt with both hands.

'Don't try anything foolish, mister, or you're dead meat!' I grated, cocking my pistol at the same time.

There was a frozen moment while he no doubt considered the odds of stabbing me before I could shoot him and having made up his mind, he lunged forward. Now the .45 Long Colt cartridge packing forty grains of black powder threw a 250 grain bullet of soft lead at about 1,000 feet per second. At a distance of five feet it threw the would-be killer back across the room, the half-inch entry hole in his chest rapidly expanding inside him to exit the size of a small teacup in the centre of his back.

He was dead and I sat shakily on the side of the bed, momentarily oblivious to the hubbub that was occurring around me as saloon staff, patrons and the general public gathered around my bedroom door.

Al Watson arrived and established some kind of order, telling the majority of the rubbernecking crowd to be gone and asking the others to remain quiet as he investigated the shooting.

'What happened, Pete?'

I gestured towards the corpse lying with open, staring eyes at the foot of my bed. 'I was lying down trying to get rid of the headache caused by the blow received earlier when this character came to my room with the intention of knifing me. I gave him fair warning but since he ignored that I shot him, as you can see. If you find a blackjack in his pocket it may turn out that he was the jerk who clobbered me last night!'

Al swiftly searched the body and sure enough retrieved a short rubber cosh, heavily weighted with lead at the business end. 'He probably thought that he had finished you off last night and finding that such was not the case decided to do the job with the knife. Any idea who he is?'

I shook my head gingerly. 'No, I've never seen him before, I'd swear to it. But wait a minute, Al! Pablo at the Cantina told me that there were two men looking for me. Get Pablo here and we'll see if he can recognize this one.' Al put a towel over the dead man's face and we waited patiently while a messenger was sent down the street to fetch Pablo. After a short while he arrived out of breath and still carrying his bar-wiping cloth, with which he now proceeded to dry his perspiring face.

Al took charge. 'OK, Pablo! Thank you for coming

131

to assist us. I want you to take a good look at this man on the floor and tell us if you recognize him.' As he finished speaking he reached down and removed the towel covering the face in a manner reminiscent of a show magician revealing his latest trick.

Pablo had bent forward for a better look at what the towel was concealing and the sudden appearance of the dead man prompted him to start back violently, muttering '*Madre de Díos*!' and crossing himself repeatedly.

Al grew impatient. 'Well Pablo? Do you recognize this man?'

'*Sí*, Señor Marshal. He came into the cantina with his friend, I thought maybe they were some kind of officials. They were asking about Señor Lomass.'

I interrupted his voluble flow of words. 'Pablo! Can you describe the other man? It is very important that we find him!'

'Well, Señores, I can try!' He thought for a long moment and finally gave us a pretty good outline of the other character. He was apparently taller than the dead man, brown-haired with a short beard. He had a small scar on the end of his nose and his teeth were very crooked. When he came into the cantina he was wearing store-bought clothing, consisting of a pin-striped suit and vest of the type normally seen in the eastern cities rather than in the West, and his hat, which he removed to wipe his brow, was of a dark brown Derby style.

Pablo next revealed to us the most startling information. When Al said to him in an off-hand way,

'Suppose you don't happen to know where they went?' the cantina owner looked at him in surprise.

'Señor Watson, they didn't go anywhere. They needed a room in which to lodge and I sent them to the widow Alvarez, you know the one whose man was killed by that runaway horse? She rented them a room. I think that they are still there. But not this one,' he corrected his statement hurriedly. 'Their horses are unsaddled in the little corral behind her house. So unless he has gone into town I think that the stranger is still there.'

I interjected. 'Pablo! Do you think that you could get Señora Alvarez out of harm's way? Perhaps if you told her your wife wanted to show her something, say, a new dress, she would come with you away from her own cottage?'

'I can try, Señor Lomass!' and Pablo set off to try and sell Señora Alvarez on the idea of going over to see the mythical dress.

CHAPTER NINETEEN

Meanwhile Al Watson and two of his deputies, together with several armed townspeople including Jim Rossiter, accompanied by a very groggy news reporter pretending to be yet another minion of the law, gathered outside the cantina waiting for word that Pablo had completed his task.

Time passed slowly until Pablo appeared accompanied by a handsomely built, raven-haired woman of middle age who appeared to take quite calmly the news that her abode could quite possibly be shot to pieces if the man in there did not surrender without a gunfight.

Silently the posse spread out surrounding the cottage and when all were in position, Al Watson produced a whistle upon which he blew a long, ear-piercing blast.

'Hey, you inside the Alvarez place! This is the law speaking! Come out with your hands up and you'll be treated decently! Make a fight of it and we'll bring you out dead!'

There was a long silence and Al ordered his men to get ready to shoot at the doors and windows. As he did so a quavering Yankee voice with a distinct nasal twang answered his original order.

'Hey youse guys out there. Don't do anyfink drastic, I ain't gonna fight! I ain't even gotta gun!' A hand frantically waving a Derby appeared at the door and upon a further instruction from Al, ventured slowly into full view trembling from head to foot.

The armed townspeople were warmly thanked and dismissed and the prisoner, surrounded by Al and his deputies, was marched down to the marshal's office and lodged in a cell. After thanking both Pablo and Señora Alvarez and suggesting that they might now be famous, I too hurried down to be present when the New York stranger was interrogated.

Unfortunately, the interrogation revealed no earthshaking revelations. Nick Schultz, aged about twenty-seven (he thought), hailed from the Bronx area in New York City. Like many kids of the area he had dropped out of school at the age of twelve, preferring to make his way in one of the many street gangs. His mother worked in a sweatshop. His father had long since departed and Nick had no idea where he lived or even what he looked like. The male figure who dominated his life was Jerry Kranz, known as Jerry the Blackjack because of his skill with laying out rival gang members and small business owners who refused to pay protection money.

Then one day Jerry had received a telegram. Now that in itself was a startling event but the contents had got Jerry all excited. Someone that he referred to as 'the Dapper' wanted his skills and was prepared to pay well to obtain them. Jerry had assured Nick that this was their big chance. All they had to do was to make one big hit together to obtain the money to pay for the trip out West. True, the Dapper had not specifically asked for Nick but his mentor insisted that everything was OK.

To get the money required, Jerry and Nick had robbed an inoffensive Jewish furrier. Unfortunately, because the man didn't immediately hand over his money Jerry got mean and used his blackjack with too much force, cracking the old man's skull like an eggshell. They were both wanted for murder!

They had left New York with the hue and cry ringing across the city, and changing trains repeatedly had made their way down into Texas where they met with the Dapper's contact man. Nick thought that it was very strange that they never met this illusive Dapper in person, especially since Jerry had insisted that he and the aforementioned Dapper were old friends.

Bert, the contact man, gave them an outline of the task. Dapper had obtained a large quantity of gold coins and had hidden them. Then some well-meaning galoot had re-hidden the money and wouldn't reveal its location. To add to the problem there were others intent on obtaining the money for themselves and they had to be eliminated.

Nick was escorted back to his cell, still boastful of his and Jerry's exploits. Apparently, he did not know that his partner was dead, and his ego was shattered when Al Watson gave him the news.

Meanwhile, Al had sent for Mr Barnard the bank manager and also George Duval, the county sheriff. Then the four of us settled down with mugs of coffee to review the whole situation to date. I opened the ball. 'I have a feeling, fellas, that I may have triggered all this series of events by coming here and making enquiries about the big town shootout twenty years ago.'

The others agreed sadly that such was the case, except for one man who sat there shaking his head. Barnard the banker disagreed. 'No, Pete, I think that we have to go back further to get at the root of the problem. Now we all know that Dapper Mike, alias Mike Carstairs and so on, was not killed in the gunfight at Ezra's corral. That fact has been established from different sources. He took off with a large sum of money which, it has now been revealed, was the true reason for all the shooting that particular night. To me it is fairly obvious that in the last twenty years Mike has spent all that money and suddenly feels the need to replenish his assets.'

We all applauded Barnard's analysis of Mike's economic problems, but Al objected. 'All you are saying, Mr Barnard, may very well be true, but that doesn't explain the shots fired at Pete here or the kidnapping of Jane Bronson to name just a couple of the problems!'

I offered my two cents' worth to the discussion. 'I think that you all should know that Dapper Mike has always fancied himself as a ladies' man. He is still wanted in New York for the death of a young lady there. In Dogleg he made improper advances to Agnes Mortimer and was soundly rebuffed. Then he tried the same approach with Jenny Ling, the little singer at Big Red's saloon and being similarly rejected proceeded to blacken the poor girl's reputation by public utterances. Then he tried to win yet another victim. I'm referring to Beth, Jane Bronson's sister. Jane told me that shortly before the shootout Dapper Mike had molested her sister, and in fact, when she recognized him, he may have shot Beth during the mayhem. That's the kind of man you're dealing with, gentlemen!

'I believe that Dapper Mike is no longer thinking rationally. I wouldn't be at all surprised if by now he was blurring the identity of Jane Bronson with that of her dead sister Beth. He probably has always seen the friendship that I've developed with Jane as a threat to his potential success in that direction, hence his attempts to get rid of me and also the note sent to Jane telling her to avoid me.'

There were murmurs of agreement as the others digested my theories as to the behaviour of our quarry and at length there was a general consensus. The talk then turned first of all to how Mike was obtaining information about what was going on in Dogleg. We were all convinced that he himself had not physically made an appearance. The town was too small for strangers to remain inconspicuous and no word of any outsider, apart from myself, had become general knowledge. We could only assume that, in addition to the mysterious 'Bert', there must be others working for him. Yet it seemed pretty obvious that with regard to his deeper plans he didn't trust his local informers, since he had sent to New York for Jerry when he needed a ruthless hatchet man.

Nick Schultz was brought from his cell and re-interrogated. No, he insisted, he didn't know anything about Bert except that he would always turn up if there was any bashing to be done. No! He couldn't or wouldn't give us any kind of description of the elusive Bert.

With regard to the murder of Old Jed he was more forthcoming. There had been two encounters with the ancient handyman. The first was where Jerry had spent the time ingratiating himself, assuring the confused man that Mr Devries had sent him to see if the gold deposit was still safe. Having convinced Jed that he, Jerry, was a legitimate messenger from the long-dead bank manager, he was furious to find that poor Old Jed had forgotten the earlier discourse and thought the handyman was holding out on him. And that was what had prompted the savage assault that killed Jed. There was nothing more to be obtained from Nick Schultz and he was returned to his cell.

The last issue – and in my opinion the most important – was the basic question, where was Dapper Mike? George Duval, the county sheriff, obtained a large-scale map from the county land office and we gathered around as he described the features and the various habitations.

'Here's the Bar 6 ranch. You should be familiar with that, Mr Lomass, and this,' tracing a line on the map with a pencil, 'is the trail to the Bar 6 where you were ambushed.' He proceeded to give us in detail each of the dwellings in the county and the statistics of the occupants.

'Now this one,' pointing to the location of a cluster of buildings northeast of Dogleg, 'is no longer a working ranch. Mrs Jensen the owner is quite elderly and wanted to go and live with her daughter in Austin, Texas. So she has leased the property to a retired army officer, a Colonel Garson, who was badly wounded I understand during the fighting in Cuba and just needed a quiet place in which to recuperate.

'I visited him shortly after he acquired the lease to welcome him to the neighbourhood and to introduce myself and let him know that if there is anything we can do to make his stay more comfortable, he should just let us know.'

I interrupted his flow of words. George Duval tended to get carried away, especially with the sense of his own importance. 'George!'

'Huh?' George Duval always spoke as though he was on an election platform and detested the notion that anyone would stop his discourse.

'George!' I repeated firmly. 'Did you actually see the colonel and speak to him man to man? If so what was his manner and how would you describe him?'

George Duval was indignant. He blustered. 'Dash

it all man! Of course I spoke to him! One of our heroes! I was very proud to have the honour of meeting him, I'll have you know!'

Al Watson was inwardly seething but spoke with slow, deliberate patience. 'George! What we would all like to know is a brief, accurate description of this Colonel Garson. Please George!' And we waited.

George, deep in thought, remained silent for a couple of minutes and then burst out with, 'Well he was a gentleman, I can tell you that! Made me sit down. Gave me an excellent cigar, produce of Havana, and also a glass of genuine French brandy. I tell you, that man is true blue through and through!'

To prevent Al Watson from literally exploding, I took up the questioning. 'George, I'm sure that the colonel has impeccable manners and you could no doubt tell us the colour of his socks but we are not after that sort of information. How tall is he? Is he fat or thin? Clean-shaven or bearded? What colour is his hair, if he has any? Is he right or left handed? Those are the sort of descriptions we are seeking. Now try again!'

He was silent, and for a moment I thought that he had retreated into his shell in a sulk, but finally he took a deep breath and responded to answer my points one by one. 'Sorry, Pete. I guess I just got carried away. Well, let us see. Height? I would say he was as tall as you, approaching six feet. He's not fat, but looks as though he lives well, like Barnard here.' Barnard looked indignant. 'He's clean-shaven. No, wait. He has a very narrow moustache, hardly discernible with his dark complexion, and hair which was carefully pomaded with some kind of hair oil.'

'Thank you, George! That is an excellent description. Now we understand that he was wounded during the late war with Spain. In Cuba, I believe you said. Would you have any idea of the nature of his wounds?'

'Well, when he rose to get me a drink I noticed that he dragged one foot as he walked across to the table where the drinks were kept. In fact he told me to come and get mine as he wasn't too steady on his pins. Oh, and one last point! When we said goodbye he shook hands awkwardly using the left hand. His right hand was apparently all twisted up, war wound you know! So he keeps it in a leather glove!'

The rest of the group looked around at each other in triumph. I was the first to break the silence. 'I think, gentlemen, we have located our man! Now we have to develop a plan to rescue Jane Bronson and capture the colonel – otherwise known, we believe, as Dapper Mike!'

'Not forgetting, Mr Lomass, that we stand a very good chance of retrieving the gold, stolen from my bank so many years ago!' As usual the banking official tended to establish a different set of priorities. Ignoring Barnard's demands that we concentrate on recovering the gold, the rest of the group considered how best to rescue Jane who, we assumed, as it turned out quite rightly, was a prisoner in the house leased by the spurious colonel. At the same time every effort must be made to arrest or put to rest the perpetrator of the murder and mayhem, namely Dapper Mike Carstairs.

CHAPTER TWENTY

George Duval, as county sheriff, was entrusted with the task of contacting the Texas Rangers and, with their assistance, putting a loose cordon around the leased property in an unobtrusive manner so that those within the ring would not be warned or alarmed.

We then debated as to who should approach the house with the main purpose of rescuing Jane. Al Watson felt that it was a civic duty for which he was well prepared. I on the other hand claimed that I knew Jane far better and if any action ensued, she was more likely to obey my instructions faster.

Furthermore, I pointed out that Al in his capacity as marshal had never actually had to draw his pistol in a gunfight, whereas I had had to fight for my life in different corners of the world in addition to the fact that I had to shoot a man intent on killing me only yesterday. I'm afraid that I laid it on a trifle thick but I was determined that I was going to be the one who rescued Jane. And so it was agreed. Al with one of his deputies would form the back-up team, in case I got into trouble.

'Al, do you have in the office a small pistol which I could use as a hide-out gun if I encounter problems?' He rummaged around in the desk drawers and in a short time produced a short-barrelled revolver with a large calibre and a box of stubby cartridges. 'Here, check this out! It's a British gun, a Webley Bulldog. Small but effective at close range. I understand they are very popular among the gamblers on the West Coast!'

I took the proffered Webley and examined it curiously. It was double action with a loading gate on the right-hand side. Cartridge extraction was by withdrawing a slender rod from the cylinder pin and then punching the empties out the same as one would with a Colt. As far as I could see, that was the only potential problem area with the little Webley. There was ample evidence to prove that these guns were effective. President Garfield had been assassinated on July 2nd 1881 by a fanatic using one of these little pistols. I loaded the short, fat cartridges into the five empty chambers, snapped the gate closed and slipped the gun into my right rear pocket, took another five cartridges and dropped them into my jacket pocket.

'There! Now I'm all prepared. Oh, there is one more thing if it can be arranged? I'd like to take Nick Schultz with me. He can identify the mysterious Bert if we encounter him.'

There were immediate protests from the others of

the group. 'He's an accessory to murder! He'll try to get away! He can't be trusted!' To all of which I agreed but I was prepared to take a chance. Nick was brought forth from his cell and I outlined my proposal to him. If he would accompany me to a certain location and would identify Bert and possibly his accomplices, then we would put in a good word for him at his trial.

After looking around the room with shifty eyes, he agreed and made a solemn promise to obey me during the expedition. We all spent the rest of the afternoon getting ready for the foray. Al arranged for the use of a touring vehicle which would accommodate himself and not one but two deputies, Nick Schultz and myself, plus all the firearms and other gear the sheriff deemed necessary. Mr Barnard departed intent on tracing the activities and movements of Old Jed, who apparently had known where the gold was hidden.

George Duval set off to contact the nearest Texas Ranger post and arrange for a loose cordon around the suspected property and I, left alone in the office, studied the map of the area and a more detailed description of the site obtained from the land office.

The house, apparently named Mount Vernon, no doubt in imitation of that house in Virginia owned by General George Washington, was a two-storey abode, fronted by a pillared portico and wide steps. Facing the front of the house, there was to the left a summer kitchen and storerooms and a similar arrangement of buildings to the right, thus creating two arms

146

either side of the main house, again reminiscent of the original Mount Vernon.

I figured that we should be able to get close by approaching obliquely through the fields, keeping the storage buildings between us and the house. After that, whether we could remain in concealment would depend on the circumstances of the moment.

We set off about an hour before sundown, Al reckoning that we could drive to within a mile of Mount Vernon and, thereafter, would have to proceed on foot, as the note of the car's engine would surely give us away.

We piled into the car, all heavily armed, except for young Nick as it was felt that giving him a weapon was putting too much of a temptation in his way. There was very little talk on the way as all the occupants were obsessed with their own private thoughts. I in particular had but one thing dominating my reasoning. What was happening to Jane? Would we be in time to rescue her from whatever fate Dapper Mike had in store for her? And how much was this hard-bitten, cynical, newspaperman emotionally involved in the potential future of this particular good-looking woman?

It would seem that but minutes had passed when the driver, one of Al's deputies, switched off the motor and let the car roll quietly to a stop. 'There you are, men! Mount Vernon is directly ahead to the right of that patch of woodland. You can just make out that darker block of buildings on the near horizon. Watch your step when going across the fields! There are drainage ditches to be encountered on the way!'

We got out of the vehicle and, with Nick and myself in the lead, followed after a short gap by Al and one of his deputies, we started off across the first meadow. The field had been used as pasture and, because of the grazing, the grass was short which made it easy for walking. On the other hand, cattle are untidy critters and one had to step very carefully to avoid the cow flaps left behind. The odd muttered curse from the rear indicated that someone had been less successful than we two in avoiding the bovine-created obstacles.

The drainage ditch could just be seen as a dark line against the sunset and we negotiated it very carefully. It was too much to just step over, being about five-feet wide and about the same depth, with a trickle of water flowing along the bottom. To get across required a degree of teamwork. I went first, hanging onto Nick's hand as he lowered me down the crumbling side. Then Al lowered Nick, who in turn got behind me and shoved as I scrambled up the far side.

In a like manner all four got across, though our pants below the knee no doubt displayed evidence of our crossing the Rubicon. We resumed our progress, with young Nick and I gradually increasing the distance between ourselves and the following pair.

The first of the outbuildings loomed ahead and suddenly, a voice challenging our right to be there spoke out of the darkness, and a powerful acetylene-powered lantern was shone in our direction, bathing us in its white light.

'You men put your hands up and come here! Don't you know that you're trespassing? We'll have to see the Colonel about you two!'

As we advanced with dragging feet, luck would have it that we separated creating a space of several feet between us. Nick, I presume, had been trying to figure out who the voice belonged to because he turned in my direction and said excitedly, 'That's him, Mr Lomass! That's Bert!'

Those were the last words he ever said as Bert's shotgun bellowed out a gout of flame in the growing darkness, throwing the man backwards like a broken doll. I, meanwhile, had thrown myself flat and rolled to the right as, simultaneously, I pulled my Colt and drew a bead on where I assumed that Bert's torso would be in relation to the lamp and shotgun.

He was momentarily put off-balance by my sudden disappearance into the darkness and he spent seconds waving the acetylene lantern back and forth, attempting to pick up my outline. Before he had an opportunity to steady his light on my prostrate form, I triggered two shots that hit their desired target, causing his shotgun to fire into the sky as his dying finger involuntarily squeezed the trigger, discharging the weapon.

I rose shakily to my feet, very conscious of the ghastly fact that I had killed two human beings in the last twenty-four hours and, walking forward, I picked up the lantern and shone it on the dead face of my latest adversary. He was revealed as a clean-shaven, nondescript person, who could pass unnoticed in any large group of people and, no doubt, walked around Dogleg without attracting attention.

Well, he certainly wouldn't be doing any more walking. My two shots, either of which could have killed him, had landed just to the left of his sternum and one at least was a heart shot.

As I was finishing my macabre examination, there was a sudden shot from the other side of the yard and I felt a stinging pain in the left shoulder as a much lighter calibre weapon was discharged. In response I threw a shot from my Colt. As the echo of the big round reverberated around the buildings, there was a squeal of fright in the darkness and, advancing rapidly, I beheld in the moonlight as the clouds rolled away a short, slender outline struggling with a pistol that turned out to be a Browning .25 calibre automatic.

'Drop it, lady, or I'll give you a much bigger dose than you gave me! Drop it I say!' These last words were practically screamed into her left ear as I rammed the long barrel of my Colt into her ribs. She obeyed instantly and, hunching her shoulders and putting her little hands over her face, she proceeded to bawl her head off.

I holstered my Colt and, although uncomfortable, did the manly thing by pulling her close and patting her thin little shoulder while simultaneously muttering, 'There, there!'

She clung to me as Al and his deputy loomed up with the former grinning as he beheld the romantic scene. My little captive had meanwhile reduced her emotional outburst to a series of large sniffs, which emerged at longer intervals as she regained her composure. Finally, when she appeared to have settled down, I felt I could obtain some logical response to the questions I put to her.

It was a sordid story. Her name was Ellen. She thought that she was sixteen. Her early life had been spent in orphanages and being farmed out to any prospective employer in need of a 'skivvy' to do unpleasant menial work. Then Mike Carstairs came along. He promised to give her a home and arrange for both an education and singing lessons.

Well, he did give her a home and had her cleaned up and suitably dressed. The education and singing lessons were continually put off as he employed her to entice elderly men to his gambling den, and even used her himself occasionally to satisfy his needs. Then it seemed that both money and Mike's temper became very short. In addition, of late, he had set his sights on getting hold of the woman that he insisted on referring to as Beth.

Ellen was ignored, that is until tonight, when he ordered her out of the house telling her to go and help Bert. Some time in the past he had given her the little Browning to protect herself in New Orleans, but had never taught her how to use it. Bert had cocked it for her so that it had one cartridge in the chamber and told her to just point it and pull the trigger.

Now Ellen was abjectly sorry that she had shot at

151

me and hoped that I didn't bear her any ill feeling. I smiled at her and did a little more shoulder-patting and then obtained from her a rough idea of the layout of the house.

The house was staffed by an ill-natured woman, Gertrude Plow, and an equally miserable husband, Hiram. She was also the cook, although Ellen claimed that her cooking skills were minimal. As to their loyalties, Ellen wasn't sure but doubted that they would fight for Mike. In fact, that had been his major complaint in recent weeks. That his gang members were deserting, like rats leaving a sinking ship he had said to Bert in a conversation Ellen had overheard. That was why he had sent to New York for Jerry. Gert and Hiram apparently kept to their own quarters unless summoned.

The house consisted of a central reception area, on the right of which was a large living room and on the left a dining room. Behind the dining room a passage led to the kitchen and scullery, while from the living room there was access to a library, office and thence to a billiard room. From the reception area a sweeping curved stairway took one to the bedrooms and a relatively modern bathroom.

As to Mike's whereabouts in the house this evening, Ellen wasn't sure but from instructions he had given to Gertrude earlier in the day, it seemed that he was going to dine with the woman he called Beth, and then spend the evening with her.

From what Ellen had told us it was obvious that Dapper Mike was becoming seriously unhinged and was mixing up Jane with her long-dead sister. It was quite possible that, by reliving the time prior to the Dogleg fire, in his twisted mind maybe he thought he could relive the bank robbery, and the stashing of the gold. Who knows what he thought? All I knew was that Jane was in terrible danger with a maniac acting out a fantasy.

CHAPTER
TWENTY-ONE

As far as we knew the shooting earlier had gone unnoticed, or was simply ignored by the occupants of the house, and we could only hope that this was because Mike was confident that any intruders had been eliminated. We crept silently up to the front of the house. There were lights on in the area that contained the dining room and a quick squint through the net-draped window revealed two people seated, having a meal.

Al and I quickly made up a rough plan of attack. Leaving his deputy looking after Ellen, he would make his way around to the rear of the house and enter through the kitchen and thence into the dining room, while I entered via the front door, checked the entrance hall and from there interrupted the two diners.

Since Al had the furthest distance to go I waited fifteen minutes before making my move. I spent the time impatiently, checking and rechecking the loads in my Colt, and ensuring that it slipped easily in my holster, while watching the luminous hands of my pocket watch move so slowly towards the appointed hour.

Time to move! I mounted the steps and passing between the painted wooden pillars, reached the front door. A twist of the door knob and the door opened silently on oiled hinges. Pistol in hand, I peered in. The entrance hall was empty, apart from a large tabby cat that regarded me sleepily from a small rug in front of the hall stand.

The door to the left led into the dining room. It was slightly ajar and creeping nearer I could just make out the murmur of conversation, though not the words. One, a male voice, was loud and hectoring then dropping to a wheedling tone as he sought to persuade his dinner companion to do something unknown.

The replies in a low, monosyllabic tone were from a subdued female whose voice I recognized instantly. It was Jane! Pushing all caution to one side I opened the dining room door and stepped in.

The first impression I experienced was one of shock. I was facing a large dinner table with but two diners present. The one closest was a well-built man, dark haired, though it was quite possibly dyed, smooth, dark features marred by a long scar reaching from the left corner of his mouth across his cheek up into his hairline. His pencil-thin moustache did not improve his slightly sinister appearance but it was the eyes that gave one the most concern. I had often read the description 'his eyes were blazing'. Well, in the case of Dapper Mike they certainly were. They glared at me with an unholy stare coupled with a cruel glint that instantly reminded me of a caged tiger I had seen in India.

It was his dinner companion who had startled me the most. It was Jane Bronson but a remarkably different Jane, dressed in the bygone fashion of a much younger person and with her hair dressed in the style of a youthful girl. Again the Jane that I knew used very little make-up to enhance her appearance whereas the figure facing Mike had cosmetics lavishly applied.

The latter broke the momentary silence that followed my entry. 'What the devil do you mean, sir, breaking into my house in this fashion?' His remark was couched in a tone of outraged indignation, and was followed by others in similar vein, all delivered in an educated East Coast accent.

At length he slowed his tirade and said, with a half smile, half grimace, 'Well, at least you can put away that awful gun. Beth here,' indicating his female companion, 'does not like firearms in any form and so we have to conform to her little weakness.' He spread his hands palm uppermost on the table in a peaceful gesture.

Gullibly, without thinking, I holstered my Colt and, immediately in a flash, he had me covered by a nickel-plated Smith and Wesson revolver drawn from a shoulder holster. He then ordered me to unbuckle my holster using one left finger and thumb and drop the belt to the floor.

'Now, Mr Clever Dick Lomass. Oh yes, I know all about you and the way you have been interfering in my affairs! So you got past my human watchdog, Bert, did you? Well Bert was too confident and no doubt has paid for it. Now it's your turn!' As he steadied his pistol on his target a sudden noise prompted him to swing wide to cover the door leading to the kitchen as the figure of Al Watson appeared.

He swung back and forth, undecided as to which of us posed the more immediate threat and I too made a choice. Keeping my eyes firmly fixed on Mike's waving pistol, I grabbed the Bulldog from my hip pocket, pointed it and squeezed the trigger three times. The small pistol bucked in my hand as it delivered its lethal load, smashing into Mike's chest and knocking him backwards to the floor.

His Smith and Wesson dropped from his fingers and the eyes were rapidly losing their fierce glare when he whispered his last conscious query, 'Why?'

I peered down at him and it seemed in accord with my quest to reply, 'Bill Syke sent me!' as his tortured soul departed to whatever destiny he had decreed for himself.

CHAPTER
TWENTY-TWO

On the way back to Dogleg, Jane described how she had been kidnapped and how, terrified, she had been forced to take on the persona of her long-dead sister. In a shed we had discovered a heavy truck, which I surmised had been used to cart away the corpse after my ambush. The housekeeper and her unsavoury spouse claimed that they knew nothing and for lack of evidence they were released.

Young Ellen was also released and arrangements were made for her to lodge with a respectable family and both complete her education and learn a worthwhile trade.

Jane and yours truly returned to Dogleg and, when a reasonable time had elapsed, she changed her last name to Lomass and sold the Eatery after making the unwise decision to follow the fortunes of a certain roving news correspondent.

Dogleg returned to being a sleepy little Texan

town and people preferred it that way. The gold was never found and I understand Mr Barnard is still searching diligently for it. Good luck to him!

As to who was responsible for writing the original doggerel that started my quest, he remains unknown but I thank him anyway since because of his scribble, I found Jane!